Apache Hostage

Apache Hostage

LEWIS B. PATTEN

Sagebrush
Large Print Westerns

Library of Congress Cataloging-in-Publication Data

Patten, Lewis, B.
Apache hostage / Lewis B. Patten.
    p.   cm.
  ISBN 1-57490-445-0 (alk. paper)
  1. Apache Indians—Fiction. 2. Large type books. I. Title

PS3566.A79 A63 2002
813'.54—dc21   2002012115

Cataloging in Publication Data is available from
the British Library and the National Library of Australia.

Sagebrush Large Print Westerns are published in the United
States and Canada by Thomas T. Beeler, Publisher, PO Box 659,
Hampton Falls, New Hampshire 03844-0659. ISBN 1-57490-445-0

Published in the United Kingdom, Eire, and the Republic of
South Africa by Isis Publishing Ltd, 7 Centremead, Osney
Mead, Oxford OX2 0ES England. ISBN 0-7531-6700-X

Published in Australia and New Zealand by Bolinda Publishing
Pty Ltd, 17 Mohr Street, Tullamarine, Victoria, Australia, 3043
ISBN 1-74030-671-6

Manufactured by Sheridan Books in Chelsea, Michigan.

Apache Hostage

ONE

AT FIVE IN THE AFTERNOON, THE THERMOMETER hanging on the adobe wall in front of the sutler's store at Fort Chiricahua, Arizona Territory, registered a hundred and fourteen degrees. At a quarter past five, the Butterfield stagecoach with its six-trooper escort, rattled and swayed down the rocky road out of the barren mountains to the east, rolled through the gates in the fort's adobe walls and ground to a screeching halt. A cloud of choking dust settled over coach, driver, shotgun guard and trooper escort with fine impartiality. The six troopers headed for the stables immediately. A couple of Mexican hostlers shuffled toward the coach to unharness the lathered horses and lead them away. No one else moved inside the fort. Every bit of shade was occupied by lounging troopers, motionless, some in soiled and sweat-stained undershirts. Faces peered out of the windows and doors of overcrowded barracks but no one came forward to open the coach door and help the passengers alight.

The air was oppressively still. A strong stench of horses, men, leather and manure hung in it, combining with the fragrant smell of smoke from cedar firewood.

The coach door opened and the passengers began to alight, wincing visibly as they stepped into the cruel brilliance of the sun. First came a gun salesman bound for Tucson, followed by an Army surgeon transferred to Fort Chiricahua from someplace in the East. Both men turned immediately to help the woman out. She accepted their help silently, then hurried across the narrow space between coach and gallery, obviously

1

anxious to get out of the sun as quickly as possible. She halted there and waited for her bag to be unloaded from the boot. Two other passengers alighted, both civilian men, both middle-aged, both dried out and burned dark by the desert sun.

Driver and guard began unloading parcels, and mail, and baggage from the boot. Finished, the driver called hoarsely, "There'll be a two-hour stop for supper, folks."

Along the gallery came a tall, gaunt officer, the armpits of his faded tunic dark with sweat. A sweeping, tawny moustache spread across his hollow cheeks. His blue eyes were narrowed against the glare.

He swept off his stained and faded campaign hat and bowed before the woman. "Welcome to Fort Chiricahua. I'm Lieutenant MacCorkindale, at your service, Ma'am."

She turned toward him. There was a film of perspiration on her upper lip. Dust had accumulated on the shoulders of her dark blouse. She let her glance rest on his face a moment, then, apparently liking what she saw, allowed a smile to touch the corners of her mouth and put out her hand to him. "I am Edith Thorne. I have come here to marry Mr. Jason Canavan. He has a ranch on Furnace Creek, which I understand is about fifty miles southeast of here."

MacCorkindale studied her, something about his previously open expression closing like a door. She was a strongly built woman, this being evident in spite of her ankle-length, voluminous skirt and long-sleeved blouse. Her face was as strong, with its high, smooth forehead, level, deep-set eyes, high cheekbones and hollow cheeks, wide and firm, though full-lipped, mouth and strong, if not overbearing, chin. He looked down at her

2

hands. They were neither large nor noticeably small. Somehow he knew they would have calluses on their palms.

He said, "Please come inside, Miss Thorne. I'll have a pitcher of lemonade brought in."

"Thank you." She picked up her dusty carpetbag, which he immediately took from her. Thereafter she preceded him along the gallery and through a door over which hung a sign reading REGIMENTAL HEADQUARTERS.

Inside the office MacCorkindale occupied as Officer of the Day, she sat in a straight-backed chair and when he offered her a glass of lukewarm lemonade, she took it with a grateful smile. There was an awkward silence that he failed to dispel successfully with small talk about the heat. At last Edith Thorne asked bluntly, "Is there something that I should know, Lieutenant? Is Jason dead?"

MacCorkindale shook his head. "No Ma'am. At least he wasn't the last I heard."

"What is it, then?"

"Well Ma'am, are you sure he was expecting you?"

"Perhaps he wasn't expecting me right now." Her face colored slightly and she looked down at her dusty, high-buttoned shoes. She raised her eyes again and met MacCorkindale's determinedly. "We had an understanding. I intended to come out next spring but— Lieutenant, please tell me what is wrong."

"Well, Ma'am, it's awkward." He hesitated, then finally plunged ahead. "Canavan's got a squaw."

She winced as though she had been struck and the color left her face. It was a long time before she could bring herself to meet his eyes. He said gently, "You'd best go back East, Miss Thorne. I don't know how much you've noticed but this fort is jammed with troops.

3

Tomorrow morning we're moving out against some Apache renegades that have broken away from the reservation. It will be a long, drawn-out campaign. You couldn't go south to Canavan's right now. The colonel wouldn't give his consent."

Her eyes now snapped. "And why should I need your colonel's permission for anything I want to do?"

MacCorkindale said, "You couldn't travel to Furnace Creek without an escort and you couldn't get an escort unless Colonel Meagher agreed."

Edith Thorne got up and began to pace back and forth. The trooper in the outer office was so silent she knew he must be listening. She also knew this was no time to let the lieutenant see either hurt or uncertainty in her. She was a woman alone in a strange and hostile land, a land where even the weather was brutal and dangerous. The fifty miles between here and Furnace Creek might as well be five hundred if she had to travel them alone.

She turned her head. Her eyes met those of the lieutenant and there was firm determination in them. She said, "You may tell your colonel that I am leaving for Furnace Creek the first thing tomorrow morning even if I have to walk."

"Ma'am, you can't do that."

"And who will stop me, Sir? Will your colonel put me behind bars to keep me here? Will he put me on a stagecoach by force? I warn you, those will not be easy things to do."

"Ma'am . . ." MacCorkindale stopped helplessly.

She said, "I was told the sutler here has rooms for travelers. I will be in one of them if the colonel wishes to speak with me."

"Yes, Ma'am." MacCorkindale stared helplessly at

4

her as she turned and went through the outer office and onto the gallery. Besides helplessness there was grudging respect for her in his eyes. He thought irritably to himself, "Canavan is a blasted fool!"

The stage pulled out at seven, with the sun hanging low over the shimmering desert to the west. Out there, giant saguaros lifted their spiny arms and in minutes the coach was only a rocking speck with a cloud of dust trailing behind.

At seven-thirty, Colonel Meagher knocked on Edith Thorne's door and when she opened it, nodded irritably at her. "Miss Thorne? I am Colonel Meagher, the commandant."

He was a short, stocky, gray-haired man with a strong jaw, bushy eyebrows and skin like leather. He had been brevet brigadier general during the War Between the States and his impatience was not altogether because of the complication Edith Thorne's presence had added to the situation in which he found himself. Rather, it was the whole concept of this endless war between the United States Cavalry and the Apache renegades that so frustrated him. Never in the history of warfare had so few been able to defeat so many so easily. He said, forcing a patience into his voice that he did not feel, "I understand you wish an escort to Canavan's on Furnace Creek."

She met his glance with her own steady one. "I have asked for no escort, Colonel. I simply informed Lieutenant MacCorkindale that I intend to leave in the morning for Mr. Canavan's ranch even if I had to walk."

"You know, of course, that you can't go unless I provide you with an escort."

"I know no such thing. I am not one of your troopers,

5

Colonel. I am a woman and a civilian. I shall do exactly as I please. I have come two thousand miles to marry Mr. Canavan. Do you think I will let the last fifty miles turn me back?"

"Didn't MacCorkindale tell you?"

"Tell me what?"

For the first time his assurance wavered. He said uneasily, "That Canavan has a squaw."

"I should think that would be a matter between Mr. Canavan and myself."

He stared at her blankly for a moment. Then a reluctant grin spread across his face. He said, "Damned if I don't think you would."

"Would what?" His grin had unnerved her and it showed.

"Walk. All right. I'll give you an escort. I'll send MacCorkindale and five troopers along with you. You can leave first thing in the morning. Does that satisfy you, Miss Thorne?"

She nodded. "Thank you, Colonel. It does indeed."

He studied her briefly, then backed out of the room. The door closed. He stood there for several moments thinking that in one respect he didn't envy Jason Canavan. He wouldn't want to have to explain a squaw to Edith Thorne. On the other hand, any man Edith Thorne wanted to marry was, in the colonel's estimation, a very lucky man.

He really couldn't spare MacCorkindale. The Lieutenant was one of his best officers. But MacCorkindale would probably catch up. He could make Canavan's in a day and then overtake the main command at Chimney Rock by nightfall of the following day. That would be their second night's camp, assuming, of course, that Chavo didn't do the

6

unexpected and head north or east instead of south and west into Sonora in Mexico.

He walked along the gallery to Regimental Headquarters and stepped inside. The trooper on duty snapped to attention and saluted him and Colonel Meagher said, "At ease, Corporal. At ease. Is MacCorkindale in there?"

"Yes, Sir."

Meagher went in. MacCorkindale had apparently heard him because he was standing behind his desk. Meagher said almost testily, "Sit down, Lieutenant. For Christ's sake, sit down. It's too damned hot for formality."

MacCorkindale sat down. Meagher walked to the window and stared out across the parade ground beyond the gallery. The sun was setting, its last rays touching the adobe wall encircling the fort. Heat waves, rising from the desert beyond, distorted the horizon and set it to wavering. Meagher thought for the hundredth time that he hated this damned place. He hated the heat, the dryness, the cactus, the rattlesnakes. Most of all, he hated the land's inhabitants, the deadly Apaches, who could travel fifty miles across the desert while the cavalry was going ten, who fought only when they chose and then at times and in places where the advantage was with them and where they could inflict losses on the cavalry with little risk to themselves. His task was going to be much more complex than simply overtaking a few renegades. He would have to force them to fight on terms favorable to him. How he would accomplish that, he had no idea.

He said, "You will take five men and escort Miss Thorne to Canavan's tomorrow. On the following day, you will head west toward Chimney Rock and overtake us there."

MacCorkindale's expression showed his chagrin. Meagher felt like apologizing to him but he was damned if he was going to. MacCorkindale was no better than anyone else in this godforsaken place. He could take orders too.

The Lieutenant said grudgingly, "Yes, Sir."

Colonel Meagher stared at him, irritated by the Lieutenant's tone. He said, "You talked to her. You know what she's like. She's liable to do exactly what she said she would—walk."

"Yes, Sir."

"She's a handsome woman. I'd think you'd enjoy spending a day with her."

"Yes, Sir."

"Damn you, stop saying that!"

"Yes, Sir. I'm sorry, Sir." MacCorkindale frowned. Then he asked, "Have you considered what will happen to her if Canavan doesn't want her on Furnace Creek? Where will she go?"

Meagher turned his head and stared out the window again. Behind him, in the outer office, he heard a match strike as the corporal lighted a lamp. Without turning he said, "If she wants to come back here I guess you'll have to bring her back."

"That will mean that I'll miss the whole campaign."

Meagher turned his head. His face was red, his eyes angry now. He said harshly, "Lieutenant, you have your orders. Don't argue them with me."

MacCorkindale, his face equally red, saluted smartly. Meagher stamped out of the office. He headed for his quarters, damning women and Apaches, thinking about the half bottle of whiskey in his bottom dresser drawer.

TWO

LIEUTENANT MACCORKINDALE'S ESCORT DETAIL OF five men fell in before the sutler's store at six. They had brought from the stables, in addition to the lieutenant's horse, a big hammerheaded gray on which there was a sidesaddle for Edith Thorne.

MacCorkindale, waiting on the gallery, turned and went into the sutler's store to get her. She was ready and came toward him at once. She was dressed in the same clothes she had worn yesterday, but today she wore a wide-brimmed straw hat for protection against the sun. Her expression was grave, a little worried, and MacCorkindale felt sorry for her. He could imagine how hard it must be for her, going to Jason Canavan knowing he had already had a squaw.

Outside again, he helped her mount. He handed her carpetbag up to Private Frank Nattress, saying, "Tie this on, trooper," then mounted his own horse and led out toward the gate.

The fort was already a beehive of activity. From the stables came the squeals of many horses, the shouted curses of many men. From the barracks kitchens came the smells of coffee and of frying bacon. Troopers were everywhere, hurrying back and forth. Three civilian scouts, two heavily bearded, lounged on the gallery in front of the sutler's store. Half a dozen Apache scouts squatted silently and impassively nearby.

MacCorkindale tried to curb his resentment at being left out of the excitement. Today he wanted to be with his own D Troop. Still, this would only take two days. He could catch up with the command by nightfall tomorrow if all went well.

9

If all went well. He turned his head and looked at Edith Thorne, surprising a forlorn expression on her face. A disquieting thought occurred to him. What if the Apaches had already been to Furnace Creek? What if Canavan's ranch was burned and Jason dead?

Maybe if he hurried they might reach Furnace Creek by midafternoon. Then, if the place had been destroyed and Edith Thorne had to be returned to the fort, it could be done by making a forced march back. Perhaps there would still be time for him to overtake the main command.

He touched his horse's sides with his heels and the animal broke into a trot. Behind him Edith Thorne's horse speeded up without urging and behind her the troopers' horses followed suit.

Southeast from Fort Chiricahua, for twenty-five miles, lay only unbroken desert. Giant saguaros marched along the horizon, their arms upraised as if in supplication to some deity. Dust rose from the horses' hoofs. MacCorkindale turned his head. "Sergeant Hurley, put flankers out."

Sergeant Dallas Hurley, bald, red-faced, sweating as if he was new to the country instead of a ten-year veteran, called, "Plummer. Whipple." And the two men split from the command to right and left and forged ahead. MacCorkindale expected no trouble this close to the fort, but Apaches were known for doing what was least expected.

The sun climbed relentlessly across the sky. As it did, the temperature steadily increased. In the shade of the gallery in front of the sutler's store it had been ninety-seven when they left at six. MacCorkindale supposed that by now it must be at least a hundred and ten here in the sun. It felt that way.

Glancing back, he saw that Edith Thorne's face was fiery. She kept licking her dry, chapped lips.

He halted his horse and swung impatiently to the ground. Leading the horse, he went back and helped her to dismount. Sergeant Hurley bawled at the flankers, who rejoined the group.

MacCorkindale showed Edith Thorne how to rest in the shade cast by her horse. He uncorked his canteen and offered it to her. She drank and handed it back, and he asked for her handkerchief which he moistened and returned. She mopped her face with it. Her flush seemed to lessen somewhat but MacCorkindale's frown remained. He hoped she wasn't going to be ill and he hoped she wouldn't faint. There was still a long way to go before they reached Canavan's on Furnace Creek.

After a ten-minute rest, he helped her remount, then mounted his own horse and led out again. Sergeant Hurley put out the flankers and urged his horse up beside that of the lieutenant. "Lieutenant, I doubt if she's going to make it, Sir. She just ain't used to this."

"She'll make it."

Hurley glanced back at her. "She's a good-lookin' woman, Sir, but what's Canavan goin' to do with two?"

"Maybe he'll get rid of the Indian."

"He don't dare get rid of her. She's the only reason he's still alive. Why do you think he took that squaw, Lieutenant? He took her so's them Apaches would let him alone. She's Chavo's sister."

"Are you sure of this?"

Hurley said, "Yes, sir. Canavan wouldn't last an hour without her. He don't dare get rid of her. Not even for this woman here."

MacCorkindale wondered if he ought to tell Edith what the sergeant had just told him. He glanced at

11

Hurley. "Where did you find this out?"

"From John Helfer, the scout."

Hurley dropped back again. Occasionally, MacCorkindale looked around to see if Edith Thorne was all right. Rocky, barren mountains loomed ahead, shimmering in the heat waves rising from the desert floor.

They reached the first of the mountains at noon. Skirting them, MacCorkindale bore slightly right. Furnace Creek came out of the mountains ten miles ahead. He could follow the creek to Canavan's.

Flankers still were out. Whipple rode to the left, halfway up the first rocky ridge. Plummer rode on the right, on the desert floor. MacCorkindale knew he should bear more to the right, giving wide berth to the mountain slope. He didn't, because he knew that would take more time, perhaps an extra hour in the next ten miles.

The heat was incredible. MacCorkindale felt as if he could scarcely breathe. He felt as if every breath he did take seared his lungs.

Edith Thorne seemed almost numb. Her face was flushed and shiny with sweat. Her blouse darkened at the armpits and down the back. The troopers behind her lounged in their saddles, making no unnecessary movements, expending no effort that was avoidable. They were used to the desert and the heat. They knew from experience that even slight exertion would drench their bodies with sweat. They also knew how excessive sweating robbed them of strength and energy.

A vague unease suddenly began to trouble MacCorkindale. He frowned and glanced at the flanker on the left. If trouble came, he thought, it would come from behind the rocks on that blistering slope. Apaches could conceal themselves where no visible cover existed. A hundred of them could conceal themselves in the rocks up there.

He turned his head, suddenly wishing he had stayed farther out on the desert floor. He beckoned to Sergeant Hurley to join him at the column's head. The sergeant trotted his sweating horse forward, raising his hand negligently in a salute. He fell in beside MacCorkindale, his expression questioning. The Lieutenant asked, "Have you seen anything?"

"No, sir. Not a thing."

"Feel anything?"

Hurley grinned. "Lieutenant, I always feel funny when I'm in country where Apaches are. Them devils can appear out of nowhere. Most times that's just what they do."

"There aren't supposed to be any down this way. They're supposed to have headed toward Mexico."

"Yes, Sir. But Apaches don't always do what they're supposed to do."

MacCorkindale continued to stare at the slope on the left. His uneasiness did not abate. It was almost as though he had seen something, some small movement, something he did not even realize he had seen. He opened his mouth to give the order to bear right away from the mountain slope—

The shot came suddenly, from the left, from directly ahead of Whipple riding along the side of the ridge. MacCorkindale stopped instantly, hand raised to halt those behind him. He saw Whipple driven out of the saddle, saw his horse bolt, dragging the trooper whose foot had caught in the stirrup. He saw the cloud of powder smoke from an Apache's large-bore gun and heard the reports of the others' guns even as he roared,

13

"Take cover! Plummer! Pull back!"

Plummer came galloping back from his flanking position on the right. Whipple's foot had come loose from the stirrup and the trooper's body lay motionless now on the rocky slope. An Apache appeared, knife in one hand, rifle in the other, and ran toward him. Hurley bawled, "Get that bastard, boys!"

A volley of gunfire erupted behind Lieutenant MacCorkindale. He didn't take time to observe its effect. He swung from his horse and turned. He caught the bridle of Edith Thorne's horse and dragged her from her saddle. Leading both horses, he pulled her, running, toward the left, toward the doubtful shelter of some clustered rocks. The other troopers ran along raggedly behind him while the Apaches darted from rock to rock on the slope, coming closer, firing occasionally at the troopers on the desert floor.

A second trooper went down. Hurley gave his horse's reins to Plummer and ran back to help. He lifted the motionless trooper and, with a great effort, slung him over his shoulder. Carrying him, he ran to the rocks where MacCorkindale and the others had taken shelter. He eased him down, but it was too late for trooper Zeitz. He was already dead, his chest a mass of blood.

Bellied down on the scorching ground behind the rocks, none of which was much more than a foot high, the remaining troopers poured rapid and excited rifle fire toward the Apaches on the slope, hitting nothing, most times not even coming close. Hurley snarled, "Damn it, don't lose your heads! Slow down and see if you can't hit one or two of 'em!"

MacCorkindale turned to look at Edith Thorne. Her face was red, sweating and dusty. She was scared but there was more than fear in her expression. She was also

14

contrite, horrified at her own responsibility for what was happening. She said to MacCorkindale, "I'm sorry! I'm so awfully sorry! Those men are dead because of me!"

He had no time to reassure her now. He returned his attention to the Indians on the slope. There must be close to twenty of them, he guessed. Seldom was more than one of them visible at a time. All but one would remain hidden, firing from behind their rocks. That one would leap up, run forward and flop behind another rock before the troopers could draw a careful bead on him.

Hurley growled, "Next time one of them devils jumps up, I want you boys to get him. Understand?"

MacCorkindale wished be could reassure Edith Thorne, could convince her that this was not her fault. It was the Army's routine job to escort civilians when there was danger from Apache renegades. But how could he reassure *himself?* He had been hurrying because he had resented being assigned to accompany her. He had skirted the mountains too closely, knowing it was dangerous, because he had not wanted to take the extra time necessary to stay safely out on the desert floor.

An Apache leaped to his feet on the slope. Instantly the guns of the troopers banged away, MacCorkindale's revolver joining them. The Indian stumbled, fell, twitched a couple of times and then lay still.

Another got up and darted toward them. The guns of the troopers opened up again, but this Apache did not fall. He dived to safety behind a rock and disappeared. Still another leaped to his feet. And now the Apaches laid down a deadly volley that killed Private Frank Nattress and put a hole in Plummer's thigh, severing an artery. Blood gushed from the hole.

15

MacCorkindale started toward Plummer, stopped when he saw Hurley crawling toward him, pulling his belt off preparatory to using it as a makeshift tourniquet. Another volley came from the rock above. Hurley collapsed across Plummer's body, blood streaming from a wound in his head.

MacCorkindale glanced at Edith Thorne. He had lost all five of his men in as many minutes. He alone was left to protect her and he knew he could not do that long against twenty well-armed Indians. He handed her his revolver, hoping she would understand what she was to do with it. She did not. She turned her attention to the Apaches on the slope, revolver held out in front of her, its barrel resting on a rock.

MacCorkindale scrambled toward Hurley to get his carbine. He reached for it, grabbed it by the barrel and drew it toward him—

The bullet striking his shoulder was like a sledge. Stunned, he heard the high yells of the Apaches as they ran down the slope. He faintly heard Edith Thorne firing his revolver, but that stopped after two or three shots. Something struck his head.

His last thought, before blackness descended, was that Edith Thorne was either dead or a captive of the Indians. He himself was dying, joining the five troopers whose lives had been his responsibility. He thought that there was no glory in this, only shame, because it was his fault and his fault alone.

Returning consciousness brought a blinding pain to MacCorkindale's head and a throbbing ache to his shoulder where the Apache bullet had struck. He heard a groan but it was several moments before he realized that the sound had come from him.

He opened his eyes upon a dazzling, blinding world, and shut them immediately, wincing against the pain. He opened them again almost at once, the lids slitted against the glare, and looked around.

Edith Thorne was gone. Hurley still lay sprawled across the body of Plummer, who now was dead. Hurley was not. He stirred, and groaned, and raised his head on which the blood of his wound had dried.

MacCorkindale sat up and raised an exploratory hand to his head. He didn't know what had struck him, a rifle barrel he supposed, but if it hadn't struck a glancing blow it would have split his skull. His shoulder was warm with blood, and stiff, but he was alive and he would stay alive. The Apaches were gone.

Hurley got laboriously to his feet. He stared around at the dead troopers. He said, "God! Holy God, they're all dead, Sir."

MacCorkindale managed to make it to his feet. He was surprised that none of the troopers had been either stripped or mutilated. Hurley said, "We got to get them back to the fort, Lieutenant."

MacCorkindale shook his head. It was beginning to look as though the Apaches had wanted Edith Thorne solely for the bargaining power she represented. They hadn't even taken time to make sure that he and Hurley were dead. They hadn't bothered to steal the troopers' mounts. All six stood waiting patiently a hundred yards away. He said, "Get a shovel off one of those saddles, Sergeant. We'll bury these troopers here."

Hurley stared at him a moment before he went after the shovel. MacCorkindale sat down on a rock and began to remove his blood-soaked shirt.

The Apache bullet had not, fortunately, broken any bones. The bullet had passed through the fleshy part of

17

his shoulder, perhaps grazing a bone as it did. That would not count for its knocking him off his feet. He walked to his horse. There was bandage in the saddlebags. He got a roll of it and began awkwardly to bandage his still-bleeding shoulder wound.

Hurley dropped the shovel and returned hurriedly to his horse. He came back carrying a brown bottle that was almost full. He gave MacCorkindale a drink, then poured some of the whiskey on the bandage. MacCorkindale winced at the burning pain.

His shoulder bandaged, MacCorkindale attended to Hurley's head wound, a deep, painful gouge over the man's right ear. Then Hurley took a drink and MacCorkindale poured whiskey over the bandage on the sergeant's head.

Afterward Hurley went back to digging. When he seemed about to collapse, MacCorkindale took over from him; between the two of them, they had four shallow graves dug before two hours passed. They buried the bodies without ceremony, knowing a detail would come back later and dig them up for return to the fort and a proper funeral. They unsaddled the dead troopers' horses and turned them loose after putting each trooper's saddle and bridle at the head of his grave. Dizzy from heat, exertion and pain, lieutenant and sergeant mounted their horses and headed south toward Canavan's.

For the first time in his Army career, the lieutenant felt desperate. He knew that if he didn't recover Edith Thorne, that career was at an end. If the Apaches killed her he would be court-martialed and drummed out of the Army in disgrace. Nor could he expect any help from the fort. Almost the entire Fort Chiricahua garrison was riding south toward Mexico, hoping to overtake the renegades. It might be months before they returned.

And even if he recovered Edith Thorne unhurt, he knew the deaths of Plummer, Zeitz, Nattress, and Whipple would be on his conscience for the rest of his life.

THREE

MacCorkindale fumed helplessly at the slowness of their pace, yet he knew he didn't dare push the horses any harder than he already was. He was almost sick with fear for Edith Thorne.

They wouldn't kill her at least, he thought. Not even Apaches kill hostages while they still have use for them. Nor would they rape her, as Plains Indians would. But they'd beat her and they'd make her work until she dropped. But—if they so much as suspected that she belonged to Canavan they'd probably kill her immediately. Scowling with frustration and with anger at himself, Lieutenant MacCorkindale continued south at a steady trot, Hurley riding about a dozen yards behind.

Canavan stared at the two riders who had been at first visible only as specks that raised a thin plume of dust along the valley of Furnace Creek. He quickly recognized them as troopers and frowned, wondering what they were doing out here alone. They must know Chavo and his renegades were on the loose.

Canavan was a solid man, wide of shoulder and deep of chest. He moved like an Indian, light-footed and silent. His eyes, calm and steady, showed little expression and were today slitted against the late afternoon sun's blinding glare. His mouth was wide, sometimes humorous, and his chin was a jutting crag.

Even after he had recognized the two troopers as a lieutenant and sergeant and noted that the lieutenant had a shoulder wound and the sergeant a head wound, he didn't move. From his vantage point behind a clump of mesquite he kept watching the valley behind them and the slopes on either side for Apaches who might be following.

Satisfied at last that the two weren't being followed, he walked to his horse, untied him and swung easily to his back. He picked his way down the brushy slope, intercepting MacCorkindale and Hurley on the two-track wagon road that followed the bed of the narrow creek.

He halted his horse and faced them, glancing only once at the lieutenant's bloody shirt. MacCorkindale said, "I'm Lieutenant MacCorkindale, Mr. Canavan. This is Sergeant Hurley. I'm afraid we have some bad news for you."

"Bad news for me?" Canavan stared at him.

"We were ambushed, Mr. Canavan. We were escorting a Miss Edith Thorne when Apaches ambushed us."

Canavan felt as if someone had struck him in the stomach unexpectedly. "Edith? Coming here?"

MacCorkindale continued urgently, "We intend to go after them, Sir, and recover her. But we needed someone who could track them and so we came for you."

Canavan stared at him briefly. Then he jerked his head in the direction of his house, farther up the narrow stream. "We'll need fresh horses. Come on."

At a trot, he led the way toward the flat-roofed, adobe

house. A woman came to the door and stood there staring at the three of them. She was dark-skinned with black hair lying in two braids down her breasts. Canavan dismounted before the door and the lieutenant and sergeant followed suit.

Canavan said, "I'll get horses." In the Apache tongue he said, "Neisha, these men are hungry." He hurried away toward the corral, leading his own horse and the two cavalry mounts. When he glanced around, Neisha had disappeared from the doorway. Lieutenant MacCorkindale and Hurley were going through the door.

Canavan's mind was in a turmoil and he was scowling angrily. He wondered how the Apaches had managed to capture Edith while the lieutenant and sergeant remained alive. He also wondered why the hell she had come without first writing him. Not that it would have changed anything. Sending Neisha back to the reservation would be the equivalent of committing suicide. He had deliberately courted her and married her according to Apache law. He had done so originally for one reason only, to make himself safe from the renegades that regularly broke away from the reservation and rampaged across the territory, killing and burning as they went.

But he had changed. He turned his head and looked toward the house again, remembering Neisha's face, her eyes, the golden color of her skin, her softness in the night. He opened the corral gate, cursing beneath his breath. Although he had to go after Edith and rescue her no matter what the cost, he could never give Neisha up. Nor could he surrender this land, into which so much of himself had gone. Three years of his life and everything he owned were here.

21

One thing at a time, he told himself. One thing at a time. He unsaddled the three horses and roped three more. He saddled them, and led them to the house.

MacCorkindale and Hurley were sitting at the table, eating. Neisha intercepted him at the door. Her English was halting but she used it now. "There is trouble?"

He nodded. " 'Paches have captured a woman these troopers were escorting—" He stopped. He had almost added, "here." He continued, "I've got to go with them."

"I will go, too."

He shook his head. "You will stay here."

He got a sack and began to fill it with food. Bacon. Coffee. Flour. Lard. Dried apples. He took two large canteens from a nail on the wall and, going outside, filled them from the stream. He took the lieutenant's and sergeant's canteens from their saddles and filled them too.

As he headed back toward the house, he stopped at the drum of horse's hoofs on the hard-packed road.

He turned his head. A man was riding up the road, bewhiskered, burned dark by the sun. He wore a dusty and sweat-stained shirt, ragged pants and Mexican sandals on his feet. He wore a wide-brimmed sombrero, the kind Mexican peasants wear.

The man stopped his horse a dozen yards away. He wore a holstered gun. It sagged lower than was normal at his side, but Canavan knew instinctively that he was no showoff. He wore the gun there because it was more convenient.

The man took off his hat and wiped his balding head with a filthy bandanna he dragged from the pocket of his pants. "Hot."

Canavan nodded. He didn't say anything, but he was

22

thinking that he didn't dare leave Neisha now. Not with this one around.

"Spare any food, neighbor?" The man's voice was ingratiating.

Canavan said unenthusiastically, "Light and go inside. There's food."

The man stared uneasily at the McClellan saddles on the two army horses. He asked, "You got soldiers here?"

"Two. That worry you?"

"Why should it worry me?" The man slid from his saddle, led his horse to the porch, and tied him to one of the posts. He approached Canavan and stuck out a grimy hand. "I'm Healey. Lemuel Healey."

"Mind saying what you're doing away out here? Apaches are taking scalps."

"When a man wants to go someplace, he goes. 'Paches don't scare me."

Canavan said, "Well, they scare me."

"How come you stay alive? You got a 'Pache squaw?"

Canavan stared irritably at him, but he took the grimy hand. The grip was diffident. Canavan said, "Go on in and eat. Wash at the stream if you're a mind to."

"I'll do that, neighbor." Healey walked to the stream, knelt and splashed water over his face. He scrubbed perfunctorily, then got up and approached the house, shaking water from his hands and wiping their palms on the sides of his filthy, ragged pants. As he went through the door, he turned his head. "You fixin' to go someplace?"

"We are."

"Mind sayin' where?"

"No secret. 'Paches jumped the lieutenant and

23

sergeant and an escort. They took a white woman. We're going to try and catch up with them."

"What white woman? Yours?" Healey pressed.

"Pretty nosy, aren't you?"

"Curious is all."

"I'll ask a couple of questions of you. Posse after you?"

Healey hesitated an almost imperceptible second before he said, "Nobody's chasin' me."

"Then why are you riding out here alone? Where you headed for?"

Healey grinned. His teeth were yellow and crooked. "Pretty nosy, aren't you?"

Canavan said, "Curious."

Healey sat down at the table, his eyes on Neisha. Lieutenant MacCorkindale asked, "Is this a friend of yours? Will he be going along with us?"

Canavan said, "He just rode in. Never saw him before. Says his name is Lemuel Healey. I figure there's a posse after him."

Healey asked, "You taking your squaw along with you?"

"I wasn't, but I've changed my mind. And you can refer to her as my wife."

"No offense." Healey grinned steadily at Canavan. "Maybe I'll go along with you."

"No," Canavan said softly.

MacCorkindale said, "He'd be an extra man, Mr. Canavan. An extra gun."

"He'd be trouble all the way."

"You don't know that, Mr. Canavan."

Canavan shrugged. He didn't particularly like riding away and leaving Healey here. He said, "All right." He stared at Healey steadily. "Any trouble and we leave

24

you, no matter where we are. Understand?"

"Maybe I don't want to go. Maybe I'll just stay here until you get back."

Canavan said, "You opened your big mouth. You'll go. Finish eating and let's get out of here."

He looked around at the interior of the adobe house. It was comfortable here. It was home. And supposing they did catch up with the Indians who had captured Edith Thorne? Supposing they managed to rescue her?

MacCorkindale and the Sergeant got up and went outside. Healey was still eating so Canavan followed them. He looked at MacCorkindale. "Did Miss Thorne know about her?" He gestured with his head toward the door of the house.

MacCorkindale nodded. "She knew."

"And she still wanted to come?"

"She said she had come two thousand miles to marry you. She said the squaw was a matter between the two of you."

Canavan walked to the corral and caught a horse for Neisha to ride. He put her own Apache saddle on the horse, then turned all the others out. He went into the house for his rife. Healey had finished eating and was staring steadily at Neisha's back. Canavan said, "Go on out and mount up. We're leaving right away."

Healey glanced at him, grinning, then got up and went outside.

FOUR

NOW, IN LATE AFTERNOON, THE HEAT WAS AT ITS PEAK. The sun seemed to sear every bit of skin it touched. The air was dead still, so hot it was difficult to breathe.

25

Canavan and Neisha patiently endured. Healey grumbled. The lieutenant and sergeant grew flushed but they did not complain.

The five rode down the bed of Furnace Creek at a walk. Before leaving the creek to turn north along the edge of the mountains, they let the horses briefly drink, and drank themselves.

Canavan first saw the plume of dust far out on the desert floor. He studied it for several minutes, before he called it to Lieutenant MacCorkindale's attention. "Somebody comin', Lieutenant. Want to wait and see who it is?"

MacCorkindale nodded.

Healey edged away. MacCorkindale drew his revolver. The hammer made an audible click, coming back. He said, "Stop right there, Mr. Healey. Let's wait and see who's coming and what they want."

Healey studied the lieutenant's face, plainly trying to decide whether MacCorkindale would shoot if he made a break for it. Canavan took his rope from his saddle and shook out a loop. He said, "He might not shoot you, Healey, but I'll dump you before you go a dozen yards. Do what the lieutenant says. Sit still and wait."

Healey settled back in his saddle, holding his horse still. Canavan edged closer, the rope ready in his hand.

The rising dust came nearer, and as it did, it held the close attention of both the lieutenant and Canavan. Gradually the figures became recognizable as two white men, civilians.

Healey bolted suddenly. Digging spurs into his horse, he whirled the animal and streaked for the creek.

Canavan was right behind him. The loop sailed out, Canavan's horse stopped, and Healey's body left his saddle. He hit the ground, skidding in the dust. His

26

horse trotted on, then stopped and turned his head curiously.

Healey got to his feet and angrily threw off the rope, which Canavan immediately began to coil. No words were spoken, but Healey's glare was murderous. Canavan rode to where Healey's mount stood. He gathered up the reins and led the horse back to where the others were. Healey dusted himself off with his hat, then followed him.

Both strangers wore wide-brimmed, floppy hats that hid their faces until they actually looked up. Both were bearded, both burned dark by the desert sun. They looked at Healey, then at MacCorkindale. "Thanks for catchin' him for us, Lootenant," one rasped. "We're obliged an' we'll be glad to take him off your hands."

MacCorkindale said, "I'm afraid not, gentlemen."

"What do you mean, you're afraid not? Healey is a murderer. He escaped from Yuma Prison a week ago an' killed two guards doin' it. He's goin' back to hang."

MacCorkindale shook his head. "Later, maybe. Not right now."

Canavan asked, "Are you prison guards? Or lawmen?"

The one who had spoken before now looked at Canavan. "I don't know what the hell business it is of yours."

Canavan glanced at MacCorkindale. He said, "Bounty hunters."

MacCorkindale said, "Apaches took a white woman from an escort and we're going after them. Healey's going too."

"Was you in command of the escort, Lootenant?"

MacCorkindale nodded, wishing he didn't feel such a guilty compulsion to justify himself.

27

Canavan asked, "Have you two got names?"

They turned their heads and scowled at him. The one who had done all the talking, a heavyset man with an oily, sweating skin said, "I'm Mike Molocek. He's Carl Pixler."

"What's the bounty on Healey?"

"A hundred."

Canavan said, "No. Not likely."

Molocek shifted slightly until he was facing Canavan. He said, "Mister, are you looking for a fight?"

Canavan felt a familiar tension coming into him. "Maybe. I don't like bounty hunters much."

MacCorkindale rode between the two. He said, "Stop it. We haven't got time for quarreling. Mr. Canavan, suppose you lead out. You two can come along or stay behind. It's up to you."

Molocek asked, "You ain't going to let Healey keep his gun, are you?"

MacCorkindale reined over against Healey's horse. He said, "Your revolver, Mr. Healey. I'll keep it in my saddlebags."

Healey seemed to debate his chances of making a fight of it. He decided they weren't very good. He withdrew his revolver from its holster and handed it to MacCorkindale, who put it into one of his saddlebags. Healey had no rifle.

Canavan led out, paralleling the barren mountains, heading north. Neisha followed immediately behind. MacCorkindale gestured for Healey to follow her and for Hurley to follow him. He fell in behind Hurley and the two bounty hunters, grumbling, brought up the rear.

The sun was now well down in the western sky. They would probably reach the site of the battle before dark, MacCorkindale thought. They might even have time to pick up the trail and follow it a ways before darkness made further trailing impossible.

His mind fought against the delay with a kind of mounting panic. He knew how far Apaches could travel in a night when they wanted to. He knew Canavan might lose the trail, particularly if a wind came up.

But MacCorkindale was a veteran. He had fought in the war. He had fought skirmishes with Apaches here in the desert. He accepted his torment over the loss of Edith Thorne as deserved punishment for being in too much of a hurry to take proper precautions against being ambushed.

But it wasn't only the loss of Edith Thorne that bothered him. He had lost four troopers too. That was, perhaps, hardest for him to bear.

Canavan maintained a steady trot in spite of the heat. MacCorkindale watched him. He wondered what, if anything, Canavan felt for Edith Thorne. He wondered if Canavan would really try to catch up with the Apaches who had stolen her. That depended, he supposed, on whether Canavan really loved her or not. But if he did not love her, why would he ask her to travel all the way out here to marry him? On the other hand, if he did love her, why would he take a squaw? Was he callous enough to take a squaw for the sole purpose of ingratiating himself with the Apaches?

Frowning, MacCorkindale shifted his glance to Neisha, the Apache woman. Hers was a straight, strong, and very shapely back. Her face, when she turned her head slightly, had a serenity, a calmness he found extremely attractive. Her mouth was full but firm. Her cheekbones were high, her nose straight and not flat like those of most Apaches he had seen. Her eyes were large and dark, her hair blue-black and smooth.

He tried to decide what it was about Neisha's face that attracted him so much. He decided it was the strength apparent there, strength that was nevertheless tempered by softness and womanliness. Canavan would be a fool to give up Neisha, thought MacCorkindale. Canavan would also be a fool to refuse a woman like Edith Thorne. MacCorkindale smiled faintly at his own inconsistency. Canavan was to be envied because he had two such women from which to choose. He was to be pitied because he had to make such an impossible choice.

Half an hour before sundown, they reached the place where MacCorkindale's patrol had been attacked. Canavan rode to the four graves and sat his horse impassively, looking down. The others grouped nearby, the horses fidgeting nervously because of the smells of blood and death remaining here. Canavan glanced up at the slope where the Apaches had been concealed. He looked at MacCorkindale.

The lieutenant said defensively, "I had flankers out," and immediately cursed himself inwardly for making any explanation at all. Canavan didn't reply. He cantered his horse in a large circle around the spot, his eyes fixed intently on the ground. He found nothing on the flat and climbed the slope. Shortly thereafter, he beckoned for the others to follow him. He had disappeared over the first ridge before Neisha, immediately behind, was halfway up the slope.

Beyond the first ridge was a shallow ravine, and beyond that another ridge. Rocks covered the ground. There was no vegetation except for the tall saguaros, the ocotillo, the prickly pear. Even these cacti were brown and seemingly dead from lack of moisture. The rocks, now in late evening, radiated all the heat they had stored up during the long hot day. Dust rose in choking clouds from the horses' hoofs.

Neisha seemed not to notice the heat. Hurley remained red of face and continued to sweat copiously. Healey sweated little, seeming to mind the heat as little as Neisha did. If he had escaped from Yuma Prison, the Lieutenant thought, he was used to heat much worse than this. The two bounty hunters were impassive and silent, watching Healey, paying little attention to anyone else. MacCorkindale wondered how big the reward for Healey really was. Canavan had seemed to think the figure of a hundred dollars was ridiculous.

A motley crew, he thought ruefully. Canavan probably didn't even want to overtake the Indians. He probably didn't even want Edith Thorne rescued from them.

And when Neisha knew who Edith Thorne was and what she was to Canavan, she wouldn't want her found any more than did Canavan.

Healey was a killer, who wanted only to escape. The bounty hunters only wanted Healey. If they had to kill him, they wouldn't hesitate. One of his severed legs, with the manacle marks still visible on it, would get them the bounty as quickly as his entire body would, alive.

MacCorkindale saw Canavan crest a rocky ridge ahead. The man turned in his saddle. He waved an arm, gesturing south, toward Mexico. MacCorkindale felt a vast relief. The renegades who had stolen Edith Thorne were heading south, probably to join up with Chavo and the others who had broken away from the reservation earlier.

That meant that this small party might be lucky enough to overtake the main command from Fort

Chiricahua.

But suddenly MacCorkindale found himself dreading the possibility. He began hoping they would not encounter the main command—at least not until he had succeeded in recovering Edith Thorne.

The trail continued south, heading toward Canavan's ranch on Furnace Creek. The sun dropped behind the horizon and the heat abated slightly when it did. Dusk crept across the land.

Canavan halted finally when it became too dark to trail. He dismounted and waited until the others had caught up. He looked at Lieutenant MacCorkindale. "No use going on."

MacCorkindale nodded. He knew the Apaches would travel all through the night. He stared at Canavan helplessly. "How are we ever going to catch up with them? They can travel all night and they can travel faster than we can."

Canavan said, "They've got to stop sometime."

"When they catch up with the main band of renegades?"

"Probably."

"Will Miss Thorne be safe?"

Canavan said, "They didn't capture her for the fun of it and they don't need women so bad they'd take that much risk just to have her for herself. They're likely planning to use her to bargain with."

"You mean they'll offer to release her if the troops turn back?"

"Something like that. Except that they won't offer to release her. They'll offer to let her live if the troops will leave them alone."

"Will they keep their word?"

Canavan nodded. "Probably. She's no good to them if

she's dead. They'll let her live but they'll make a slave of her. They'll work her until she drops and then they'll probably beat her because she can't work any more."

MacCorkindale met Canavan's eyes determinedly. He said, "It's my fault. I didn't want the duty of escorting her. I wanted to be with my troop when they moved out against that band of renegades."

"What's that got to do with it?"

"I knew we ought to stay farther out on the desert floor. I knew skirting the mountains was dangerous."

Canavan studied him briefly. His eyes were impassive, neither showing condemnation nor sympathy. He asked shortly, "Do you think you're the only man who ever made a mistake?"

"Mine cost four lives."

"I guess that's something you'll have to settle with yourself. I can't help you out."

MacCorkindale felt his anger flare. He stared irritably at Canavan. Canavan turned away.

MacCorkindale's shoulder was aching savagely. Sergeant Hurley, his eyes narrowed against the pain in his head, unsaddled his horse and sat down on the ground, holding his horse's reins. Canavan stretched a picket line between two tall saguaros and tied his and Neisha's horses to it.

MacCorkindale led his own horse and Hurley's to the picket line. Neisha already had a small fire going. The bounty hunters stayed close to Healey, tying their horses when he tied his, following him back to the fire afterward. MacCorkindale stared gloomily at the dancing flames. Justifying what had happened was impossible. The time would come when he would have to accept the consequences. In the meantime, he had to recover Edith Thorne if that was possible. He had better concentrate on that and do penance for his mistake afterward.

FIVE

NEISHA COOKED FOR CANAVAN, MACCORKINDALE and Hurley. Healey, scowling, cooked for himself. Pixler waited until the others had finished before cooking supper for Molocek and himself. Afterward the fire started to die down. Molocek approached the lieutenant. "Healey ought to be tied up, Lieutenant. If he ain't, he's goin' to get away."

"Then tie him up."

"Manacles all right?"

"If you've got any."

Molocek got a pair of manacles from his saddlebags. While Pixler held a gun he manacled Healey's right wrist to his left ankle. Healey could lie down comfortably but it would be literally impossible for him to get on a horse.

Canavan said, "I'll stand guard, Lieutenant. You and your sergeant need the sleep. I can call one of those bounty hunters at midnight."

"We can't trust them."

"Neisha can stay awake."

MacCorkindale nodded. Canavan moved away from the camp, taking a position in some rocks slightly higher than the camp. Neisha went with him, carrying blankets, and spread them on the ground. She did not lie down or at tempt to sleep. Speaking in the Apache tongue, Canavan said, "Something's troubling you."

"Yes. This woman—where was she going?"

He hesitated, then decided it was time to tell the truth.

34

"She was coming to me."

"She is related to you?"

"She was going to marry me. It was arranged a long time ago before I met you and married you according to Indian law."

"You will have two wives?"

He frowned in the darkness, glad she couldn't see his face. Her tone had been hurt, but there had been acceptance in it too. He said, "No. White men are not permitted to have two wives."

There was a long silence after that. Canavan cursed softly to himself. He had told her clumsily and had hurt her, something he had not meant to do. Neisha lay down on the blanket silently. He knew her eyes were closed. He also knew she would not sleep, not for a long, long time.

But what could he tell her that would reassure her? He didn't know himself what he would do. He had not expected Edith yet, but he had made arrangements with her to come. He had fully intended to marry her. He tried to visualize her face in his mind but it eluded him.

He could hear Neisha breathing softly on the ground. He stared beyond at the dying fire, at the lumped shapes of men around it. He heard the fidgeting of the horses on the picket line.

He wanted to lie down beside Neisha, to draw her close to him. She would not resist if he did, he knew. But it would be different. She would show her fear that he would send her back to the reservation, fear that he would send her away from him.

Could he send her away? He shook his head angrily. He didn't know. If he did send her back, he would have to leave the ranch on Furnace Creek. The Apaches would burn it. They would kill him if they found him

35

there.

But aside from the ranch, could he bear to give Neisha up? And if he did not, how could he condone the wrong he had done to Edith Thorne? He had told her he wanted to marry her. She had come out here relying on that promise and had been captured by the Indians. Even if she lived, the ordeal would leave indelible scars on her.

He got up and began to pace nervously back and forth. He could feel Neisha's eyes watching him. He wished he could tell her that he wanted only her but he couldn't bring himself to say the words.

Down by the fire, someone began to snore. Canavan stared moodily at the lumped, sleeping shapes. The fire had died to a dull red glow. The sky was wholly dark.

On silent feet, Canavan moved away. Stepping as carefully as any Apache Indian, and making as little noise, he made a big circle of the camp, sometimes stopping to listen to the wind, sometimes stopping to sniff the air like a hound. When he returned to Neisha, she was lying in the same position. He knew she was wide awake. He asked softly, "What will they do with her?"

Her voice did not answer immediately. At last she said, "They will keep her. You cannot get her back. They will use her to force the soldiers to go back to the fort. They will threaten to kill her if the soldiers do not return."

"And if the soldiers do go back?"

"Perhaps they will kill her then. Unless one of the men has taken a fancy to her."

"What if we try to get her back?" He didn't really have to ask. He knew the answer. But he wanted to hear it from her.

"They will kill her before they will give her up."

He said, "Go to sleep. I will wake you at midnight. You are to watch the bounty hunters and wake me if they try to take Healey and escape."

She did not speak after that but he knew she did not, immediately, go to sleep. He sat staring moodily at the sky and the desert for a long, long time. The heat had not abated appreciably. It would not begin to cool before midnight.

At midnight, he got up stiffly and descended to where the others were. He stood over Pixler and said, "Get up. It's your watch."

Pixier sat up. Canavan supposed the man was a light sleeper. Or else he had not been asleep at all. Pixler pulled on his boots and picked his rifle up. He walked to where Healey lay and stared down at him. Then he packed a pipe, lighted it and began to pace silently back and forth.

Canavan returned to the rocks where Neisha was. He touched her and said, "Stay awake. If anyone but Pixler moves down there, wake me."

She got up and Canavan lay down. The air was cooler now. The blanket was warm where she had lain. He closed his eyes, and was almost instantly asleep.

Neisha was like a statue, as unmoving as the rock upon which she sat. Her eyes were on Pixler pacing back and forth beyond the dead fire. She could hear Canavan's regular breathing almost at her feet.

She found herself hoping that the Apaches who had captured her would kill Edith Thorne. It was a possibility. They were traveling fast and they would not permit her to slow them down. She would keep up or she would die.

What kind of woman was she, Neisha wondered? Was she gaunt and bony and angry looking like so many of the white women who lived out here? What did she bring to Jason Canavan? Could she guarantee his safety from Apache renegades? Could she ride as Neisha could? Could she give him help with his cattle and his hay when there was need of it? Could she give him a child—?

Neisha put a hand on her belly. It was only slightly larger than before but sometimes she could feel a slight movement there. She smiled faintly, thinking of the child, and then the smile faded as she thought that he would be half brown and half white, what the white men called contemptuously a "breed".

That would not matter, she thought. They lived on Furnace Creek and they seldom saw white men. He would be a beautiful child with a strong, straight body, and his face would be like Jason Canavans with its jutting jaw and strong, flat-planed face and deep-set eyes, as brown as any Indian's eyes.

But what if Jason Canavan took Edith Thorne as his wife and sent Neisha back to the Indians? What would then happen to the boy?

She had not yet told Jason Canavan that he was going to have a son. Nor would she tell him now. She would save that news for the time when the choice between Edith Thorne and herself had to be made.

Pixler stopped pacing down below, instantly drawing her attention. He stirred his partner, Molocek, with a toe.

Molocek rose silently. He went to where Healey lay, knelt and hit the sleeping, manacled man on the head with the barrel of his gun. Pixler was already at the picket line and the horses were fidgeting . . .

She hesitated only a moment, weighing what the departure of the three might mean to the chances of recovering Edith Thorne. Their leaving would mean the lieutenant would have three less men when the showdown with the Apaches came. But Canavan had told her to wake him if the three tried to get away . . .

Reluctantly she knelt and touched his shoulder. He came instantly awake. She said, "The other bounty hunter is awake. I think they mean to take the prisoner and leave."

He was immediately on his feet, moving away silently. Seconds later she heard his voice, harsh and angry say, "Go back to sleep, you two. I'll take over for the rest of the night."

Molocek, still standing beside Healey, who was now unconscious from the blow, cursed softly. He said, "You son of a bitch, you can go to hell. We're takin' Healey and we're takin' him right now."

Fear touched Neisha, fear for Canavan. She began to hurry toward the group below.

Canavan bawled, "Neisha! Stay back!", but it was too late. Pixler, who had left the picket line, now came running toward her. She understood that he meant to use her as a hostage, and immediately whirled away. Canavan's gun flared, and Pixler stopped.

MacCorkindale and Hurley now were awake. Molocek raised his hands and a moment later so did Pixler.

Canavan said, "Just shuck your guns, you two, and step away from them."

Their guns thudded to the ground. Canavan gathered them up. He gave them to Sergeant Hurley, who put them in his saddlebags. He said, "We'd better not trust those two again, Lieutenant. They knocked Healey out

39

and they were getting ready to haul him away."

Neisha stared at the two bounty hunters bitterly. She had been a fool. She should have let them go. The lieutenant was wounded and the sergeant was too. Canavan and two wounded soldiers would never be able to recover Edith Thorne.

She should have let the bounty hunters go but it was too late now. The lieutenant had their guns.

SIX

THEY MOVED OUT AT DAWN, AGAIN WITH CANAVAN in the lead following the Apache trail. He could tell from the tracks that the Indians were not hurrying. They had no way of knowing they were being trailed and he did not intend to let them know.

The desert shimmered in the rising waves of heat. Mountains, bare and rocky, rose on both sides, almost lost in the vast distances.

Healey squinted painfully against the glare. Occasionally he raised a hand to his head to gingerly explore the bleeding gash put there by Molocek's gun barrel the night before. He winced sometimes with pain.

Molocek and Pixler remained sullenly silent. At each stop, they moved away and conferred together in lowered tones. Canavan supposed they were trying to figure out some way to get back their guns. After that they'd like to take Healey and head for Yuma and the reward waiting for them there.

Lieutenant MacCorkindale quite obviously chafed at the slowness of their pace even though he must have been aware that faster travel would be self-defeating in the end.

Canavan frowned worriedly at the direction the trail was now taking, bearing east toward the mouth of Mexican Creek. There would be a trickle of water in Mexican Creek at this time of year, and he hoped that was all the renegades were interested in. Sam Flores had a ranch on Mexican Creek which he occupied with his wife and four children. Maybe the Apaches would be satisfied with watering their horses in the creek. Maybe they would not.

He stepped up the pace to a trot, straining his eyes ahead, seeing nothing but the mirages caused by rising waves of heat and the distorted line of rugged mountains now straight ahead.

Glancing back, he saw that Hurley's face was gray. The man was still suffering from the bullet wound on his head and neither the heat nor the motion of his trotting horse had helped. MacCorkindale was also suffering from his shoulder wound which still bled enough through the bandages to show bright red. MacCorkindale cantered his horse to the head of the column, face white, jaws clenched against the pain. He looked at Canavan questioningly and Canavan pointed toward the line of mountains barely visible ahead. "They've changed directions, Lieutenant. They're headed east toward Mexican Creek."

"Why?"

"There's water in Mexican Creek and there's a little grass. There's also a ranch—*that's* what worries me."

"Do you think they'll attack the ranch?"

"I'm hoping not. I'm sure hoping not. But that's why I speeded up. If they know we are trailing them maybe they won't feel like taking the time to bother Sam Flores and his family."

"If they know we're trailing them, we'll lose them,

41

Mr. Canavan. Have you thought of that?"

"Right now I'm thinking about the Flores family. Sam and his wife have four kids. I wouldn't want anything to happen to those kids."

MacCorkindale didn't protest any further. He dropped back in line. He spoke to Hurley, explaining the need for haste.

Canavan could see the cut in the mountains, now, where Mexican Creek emerged onto the desert floor. He strained his eyes, looking for traces of smoke in the air. The distance was too great and he knew it, but he kept staring anyway. Perhaps the Apaches only wanted water and grass for their horses. Perhaps they'd let the Flores family alone. Perhaps . . .

Another half dozen miles fell behind. The sun now hung halfway down the western sky. The heat was like that coming from an open furnace door. Nothing moved in the desert, no bird, no snake, not even a lizard.

Then Canavan saw it, a thin plume of smoke that he tried to convince himself was imaginary. But he knew it was real enough. He knew it came from the Flores ranch.

The barn, he thought. Oh Lord, let it be the barn. Maybe Sam saw them coming and holed up in the house with his family. Maybe he managed to drive them off. He couldn't keep them from firing the outbuildings, but maybe he'd managed to keep them from firing the house.

Knowing it was foolish, but unable to help himself, Canavan urged his horse into a lope, and the animal responded.

Ahead the rising smoke was plainer now. Canavan began alternately to curse and pray beneath his breath. Neisha kept pace with him, but the others gradually

42

began to fall behind. He didn't care. Neither MacCorkindale nor Hurley had ever met the Flores family. Healey certainly wouldn't care what happened to them. Nor would the bounty hunters care.

But Canavan did. Between Sam Flores and himself had existed a bond born of facing common peril every day. He hadn't seen Flores more than half a dozen times in the last two years. That didn't seem to matter. What did matter was that they were two alone against this hot and hostile land, against the incredibly savage Apaches who would hold it against the white invaders if they could.

He turned his head and looked at Neisha once. She was not looking at the rising smoke. She was looking straight at him and there was compassion in her eyes. She knew how he felt about the Flores family. She also knew what must have happened to all six of them.

Canavan was galloping when he struck the two-track road that followed Mexican Creek to the Flores ranch a mile beyond the first ridge of mountains that rose from the desert floor.

A single glance at the dusty road told him the Apaches had been and gone. The tracks were fairly fresh, perhaps not more than an hour old. But he didn't take time to dismount and study them. Time was important now. Perhaps some members of Sam Flores' family were still alive.

Rounding a shoulder of jutting rock a quarter mile below the ranch, he saw that smoke was rising from all the buildings. The house was still burning, indicating that it had been the last of the buildings to be set ablaze. The barn was a pile of blackened timbers. Some of the smaller outbuildings were only smoking piles of ash. The corral was empty. A milk cow lay dead not far from the back door of the house. A few white chickens scratched in the dusty yard.

Canavan didn't slow his horse until he was several yards from the blazing house. He swung to the ground, knowing Neisha was just behind, and ran toward the first of the still figures lying scattered about so carelessly.

It was the body of Sam Flores' wife, dark of skin, black of hair and eye, buxom and, in life, motherly. She was dead now. He knelt and carefully closed her eyes.

Something had caught and tightened in his throat. He felt a raging, helpless anger against the Apache savages. Sam Flores had taken nothing the Apaches used. He had never raised a hand against them in his life. But they had done this anyway, like cruel children who, when hurt, strike out at everything in range.

The second body was that of a child. Canavan stood looking down, recognizing the child as Davis, the oldest of the four. Canavan's face twisted; he went to the next, the body of Maria, only three years old. Her head had apparently been smashed against the wall. Then Joseph, recognizable only by his size. He must have been hit squarely in the face. The baby, Elena, lay closest to the house. Her baby clothes were smoking, scorched by the heat of the flames. Canavan picked her up and carried her back to where her mother lay. Sam Flores lay sprawled down by the corral, staring at the sky.

Canavan was talking to himself but he didn't realize it until he saw Lieutenant MacCorkindale staring strangely at him. He turned his head furiously. "God damn it, what's the matter with you? These were my friends."

MacCorkindale said contritely, "I'm sorry, Mr. Canavan." He turned his head and looked at Molocek,

44

Pixler and Healey. "Find something to dig with, you three. We'll need six graves." Turning back to Canavan he asked, "Do you have any idea where Sam Flores would have wanted the graves to be?"

Canavan gestured toward the barren hillside, where giant saguaros rose above the rocks. "Up there someplace."

The bounty hunters poked around the yard. They found two shovels. MacCorkindale said, "Sergeant, go with them."

"Yes, Sir." Hurley followed the three across the narrow valley and climbed the hillside behind them, rifle ready in his hands, enough distance between them and himself so they couldn't rush him in an attempt to get his gun.

Canavan thought about Edith Thorne for the first time today. She had been forced to witness the murders here. He felt a sudden compassion toward her. It must have been terrible to have to watch Flores, his wife and four little children slaughtered like animals.

He had never really hated the Apaches before today. He had feared them and respected them, but always beneath his feelings toward them had been a grudging sympathy. White men had lied to them, cheated them, slaughtered them, captured them and penned them up. He didn't blame them for fighting back. But this wasn't fighting back. Slaughtering children and babies wasn't fighting back.

There was a pile of cedar logs on the far side of the yard. Canavan crossed to it and sat down on a log. He was sweating heavily. His arms and legs were trembling. He licked his dry and cracking lips.

He was mad. He was raging mad. He still had to try and get Edith away from those savages, but now there

45

was something else he intended to settle with them. They weren't going to get away with this—not if he had to track them down one by one and exact personal vengeance for this atrocity.

Neisha came across the yard. She sat down silently at his feet. He looked at her, briefly aware that she too was Apache, kin to the savages who had murdered here. She glanced up, saw the thought in his eyes, and averted her eyes as though accepting a share of the guilt.

Impulsively he put out a hand and rested it on her shining hair. He said, "I'm sorry. It's not your fault, any more than Healey and Pixler and Molocek are mine."

"What will you do now?"

"Go on. This doesn't change anything. They still have Edith Thorne and we have to get her back. I'm going to enjoy it now. I'm going to enjoy what we do to them."

She turned her head and looked up at him soberly. "These are not the Apache people I know any more than those three up on the hillside are the white people you know. These Apaches we are following are the wild young ones that even the chiefs cannot control. They are like mountain lions who have tasted blood and who thereafter must gorge themselves on it."

He managed a thin smile. "You don't have to tell me that. I know. Seeing Sam and his family lying around like this—well, I just couldn't handle it right away."

Up on the hillside, Molocek and Pixler were digging. Canavan walked up the steep slope toward them, followed by Lieutenant MacCorkindale. The ground was rocky, but it wasn't hard. Canavan said, "Make them two feet deep. We don't have time to dig them any deeper than that."

It was hard to suppress his anxiety to be on the trail again. He wanted to be riding; he wanted to dig spurs

46

into his horse. He wanted to catch the renegades before the sun went down. That was impossible and he knew it was. He couldn't catch them immediately. Even if he could, he couldn't risk Edith's life by openly attacking them.

The shovels made metallic sounds striking rocks in the dry, sandy soil. Sweat had soaked the clothes of both Pixler and Molocek. Their faces gleamed with it. Both of them were breathing hard.

Canavan said, "Take a rest," and climbed into one of the graves. Hurley relieved the other bounty hunter. The two sat in the thin shade cast by a saguaro, breathing hard.

Exertion helped dull the pain in Canavan's thoughts. He worked until he was bathed with sweat. He finished one grave, began another and finished it. He was unaware of the others until he heard MacCorkindale shout, "Take a rest, Mr. Canavan! You'll kill yourself!"

He climbed out of the grave. He rested briefly in the shade of the saguaro, then got up and walked down to the Flores yard. He lifted Mrs. Flores, laid her body on his horse and led the horse up the hillside to the graves. He carried her to one of them and let her roll into it because there was no other way. He went back for Sam Flores. Lieutenant MacCorkindale brought two of the children, then went back for the other two.

All the graves were finished now. The sun hung low in the western sky. Canavan looked at Pixler and Molocek. "Get out of here and take your escaped prisoner."

They scowled at him. Pixler muttered, "We're good enough to dig their goddamn graves, but not good enough to stand here while you bury them. Is that it?"

Canavan said savagely, "Shut up and get out of here!"

They walked down the hill, Hurley behind them, his carbine ready. MacCorkindale asked, "Want me to go with them?"

"No. I'd like you to stay."

Neisha started to leave, but Canavan called her back. The three stood looking down at the unfilled graves, one of which was scarcely more than two feet long. Canavan cleared his throat. He said, "These were good people, Lord." He groped for something else to say without finding it. He looked helplessly at MacCorkindale, who also groped for words and finally said, "The Lord giveth and the Lord taketh away. Blessed be the name of the Lord."

Canavan growled something beneath his breath. He picked up a shovel and began working furiously, filling in the graves.

MacCorkindale picked up the other shovel. When the graves were filled in and carefully mounded over, the three walked back down to the gutted ranch. They mounted and Canavan led out toward the south, his face set in a grim, forbidding mold.

SEVEN

THEY CAMPED TEN MILES FROM THE BURNED-OUT ranch when it became too dark to follow even the plain trail left by the Apache horses. It was a dry camp, but the horses had been watered earlier in Mexican Creek and all the canteens had been filled. Neisha built a fire and made coffee for Canavan and for herself. Hurley built another small fire upon which he cooked bacon and made coffee for himself and for Lieutenant MacCorkindale. The bounty hunters and Healey moved off by themselves, but several times Canavan caught Healey staring at Neisha broodingly.

Another man might have suspected that Healey's stare was caused by anger at the Apaches over the killings on Mexican Creek. Canavan knew those brutal murders had left Healey untouched. He knew why Healey was watching Neisha. He had been in Yuma too long, and in all that time had not been near a woman, Indian or white. He was dangerous to her, but Neisha didn't seem to be aware of him.

Again this night Canavan took the first watch. Tonight he called MacCorkindale at midnight, and afterward lay down with Neisha in the bed that she had made. She lay rigid and still, not touching him. He supposed she thought he and the others were blaming her for what the Indians had done to the Flores family, but he was too tired to think about it now. He closed his eyes and was almost instantly asleep.

MacCorkindale awakened him at dawn. He sat up groggily. Neisha was already up. She had a fire going and coffee ready for him.

He pulled on his boots and gulped a cup of the scalding stuff. He chewed some pieces of Indian jerky from Neisha's saddlebags. He led out just as the sun was coming up.

Again, every time he turned his head, he became aware of Healey, staring at Neisha with slitted eyes. Each time he felt anger stirring in him. Healey was filthy and unsavory. He had killed two guards escaping the prison. He had killed before that or he would not have been in prison at all.

Today they were not as far behind the Apaches as they had been yesterday. Canavan guessed the Indians were no more than a dozen miles ahead. They could close that gap at any time. But what if they did? The Apaches outnumbered them and they didn't dare attack or Edith was certain to be killed.

So he held the same distance all through the day, traveling at a relatively easy pace. At nightfall, they dry-camped again, in rocky, rolling country cut by deep arroyos surrounded by tall, browning saguaros, some of which had died from lack of water over a prolonged period.

MacCorkindale seemed feverish tonight. Canavan made him sit on a rock, and unwound the bandages from his shoulder wound. They were stuck together with blood and he had to cut the last of them away.

The wound was festering. He washed it thoroughly with water first, then with whiskey from a bottle Hurley carried in his saddlebags. Hurley also had fresh bandages and Canavan wound them around the lieutenant's shoulder, but not as tightly as before.

MacCorkindale's face had turned ashen. A couple of times, Canavan had to steady him. When he had finished, he told MacCorkindale to lie down. Hurley insisted that the lieutenant take a pull on the bottle before he did.

The sun had been down fifteen or twenty minutes. Canavan looked at Hurley's head wound. He decided it would heal as well without bandages as with them and so did not rebandage it.

In the first gray light of dusk, he straightened and looked for Neisha. He didn't see her and supposed she had gone for firewood. He stared to sit down, but stopped when he noticed that Healey was also gone.

He glanced at the bounty hunters. "Where's your prisoner?"

Both of them shrugged unconcernedly. "There's his

horse," Pixler said. "He ain't goin' far without a horse."

Fear touched Canavan. Neisha was gone and so was Healey. Remembering the way Healey had been watching her all day he knew that the man must have followed her when she left to look for firewood.

How long had the two been gone? And if Healey had caught her, why hadn't he heard her scream?

He knew the answer to that. Apache women do not scream. Neisha would fight her own fight with Healey and if she lost—

He hurried away from camp. He made a swift circle of it, and almost immediately picked up the tracks of Neisha's moccasins, in places overlaid by the tracks of Healey's Mexican sandals. He began to trot, the easy, tireless trot of an Apache, eyes on the ground, face impassive and not revealing the terror in his mind. He knew that Healey might already have overtaken her. Neisha might be dead.

Why hadn't he kept an eye on her? Why hadn't she told him she was leaving camp? He knew the answers to both questions. He hadn't kept an eye on her because he'd been busy with Lieutenant MacCorkindale. She hadn't told him she was leaving because she hadn't thought it necessary.

He found several places where she had picked up firewood, or where she had broken off dry branches of mesquite. A little farther on he found where she had dropped her armload and here the tracks told him she had begun to run.

Healey's tracks, following, were deeply indented, and widely spaced. Canavan, terror growing in his mind, now also began to run.

It was rapidly darkening. Soon he'd have to slow to a walk because of difficulty in seeing the ground. But they couldn't have gone far beyond this place. Neisha could run for a long way, but Healey could not. Healey, faster because of his longer legs, would have had to catch her almost at once or she would have escaped.

How long had they been gone and how far ahead of him were they? He began to glance up at frequent intervals now, trying to pierce the gathering darkness ahead of him. He realized he was listening . . .

He heard it suddenly, a grunt of exertion from almost directly ahead. Fury flared in him like a fire upon which gunpowder has been thrown. He didn't think about his gun. He didn't think of his knife. He could only think about getting his hands on Healey's filthy throat.

Suddenly, almost immediately ahead of him he saw the two of them. They were locked together on the ground, struggling. Neisha was fighting silently, but with a stubborn fury. She knew that to surrender was to die.

As Canavan came in sight, Healey suddenly began hitting her with his fists, trying to subdue her, trying to knock her out.

Canavan reached the two with a last furious burst of speed. He aimed a running kick at Healey's head and knew a fierce satisfaction as it connected and sent Healey rolling away.

Neisha came to her knees, clothes torn, mouth bleeding and bruised, hair in disarray. Canaven looked at her, unable to see her expression because of the darkness. He said, his voice soft but charged with fury, "Go back to camp."

"Jason—"

"Go back to camp."

"I didn't—He didn't—"

"I know. Now go back."

52

"Yes, Jason." She turned and disappeared into the darkness in the direction of the camp.

Healey was on his hands and knees, shaking his head as though to clear it. Canavan faced him with an unfamiliar eagerness. He *wanted* Healey to get up and come rushing at him. He *wanted* to batter the man into insensibility with his fists. He had been in many fights, but never had he experienced the vengeful anticipation he was feeling now. His voice was soft. "Get up you son of a bitch! Let's see if you're as good fighting men as you are fighting women!"

Healey said thickly, "You got a gun."

"And maybe I'll use it before I'm through."

Healey came cautiously to his feet. Canavan understood what was in the convict's mind. If he won, the spoils would include his adversary's gun. With it, he might manage to kill the two bounty hunters and escape.

Slightly crouched, arms spread, Healey came toward him. Canavan didn't wait. He moved toward the convict, aware of the rapidly fading light. In minutes, no more than five or ten, it would be completely dark. Darkness would make the outcome of the fight less predictable. It would favor Healey if it favored anyone.

Less than fifteen feet from Healey, Canavan rushed, overcome by anger. He drove against Healey with a shoulder that struck the convict in the belly, driving a helpless grunt from him. Healey was bowled back by the force of his charge, but even as he was, Canavan felt the man's hand clutching for his holstered gun.

Again Healey struck the ground on his back. This time Canavan was on top of him immediately. He came down with both knees in Healey's midsection, and felt the crack of at least one rib. That gave him a fierce satisfaction. He rolled on past, again feeling Healey's

53

hands clutching for his gun.

He came to hands and knees, startled and surprised by the speed with which Healey had regained his feet. The man was gasping for air, aiming a murderous kick at him as soon as he was in range. Canavan threw himself to one side and Healey's foot grazed the side of his head. Canavan's hand came down squarely in a clump of prickly pear and the spines burned as though he had stuck it into a bed of coals. Enraged by the thought of hundreds of cactus spines in his hand, he came to his feet and stood there, panting and this time waiting for Healey to come on.

Once more Healey approached in a slight crouch, arms and hands outspread. Canavan knew he ought to draw his gun and stop Healey where he stood. He was a fool to fight it out this way.

Too late, he saw that Healey had rocks in both his hands. Healey swung at him with his right hand first. It missed, because Canavan ducked, but immediately, Healey's other hand came around, and this time the rock grazed the side of Canavan's head.

The blow stunned him and knocked him back. He sat down heavily. With a sound like an animal's growl, Healey plunged toward him to finish him. His right hand, containing the largest of the two rocks, was raised above his head like a club.

Perhaps desperation lent speed to Jason Canavan. Perhaps it also cleared his head. He fell back, raising both feet as he did. When Healey swung, throwing himself forward to give added force to the blow with which he intended to brain his adversary, Canavan kicked out at him. One foot missed, but the other connected squarely with Healey's jaw.

There was a meaty sound to the kick, and Healey

came down on hands and knees, stunned and nearly helpless. Jason got up and kicked Healey in the side of the head. Still the man did not go down so he swung a haymaker with his right fist that landed squarely on Healey's ear.

Healey went over and lay there breathing hard. Canavan started to turn away. Too late, he realized his gun had fallen from its holster a moment before when he had sat down so suddenly. He turned to retrieve it in time to see Healey's hand close over it.

He knew a moment of panic. He had indulged himself battering Healey with his fists and there had been satisfaction enough in it, but he had been a fool. Now he was going to die for his foolishness. In seconds Healey was going to shoot and that would be the end.

Frozen, he stood, staring at the gun in Healey's hand. He heard the hammer click as Healey drew it back. He saw the blur of Healey's arm and the fisted gun rising, coming into line—

He could throw himself aside as the gun lined up but beyond that there was little he could do. He tensed himself, and when the gun came into line, flung himself aside.

The muzzle blast seemed to be almost in his face. Concussion deafened him and grains of powder burned his face, feeling like grains of blowing sand. The bullet missed, the first bullet at least, but he kept rolling, frantically trying to keep moving so that Healey couldn't draw a steady bead.

A second shot roared and this bullet showered Canavan with dirt. The next would get him, he thought, and there wasn't a damned thing he could do about it.

Behind him, he heard a solid, chunking sound. No third shot came. He stopped rolling and stared toward

55

the place where Healey had been only moments before.

Neisha was standing there, a twisted length of firewood in her hands. Healey lay unconscious on the ground. Canavan heard the sounds of running feet and approaching voices, and got up. He went back to where Neisha stood over the unconscious form of Healey and quickly retrieved his gun.

The bounty hunters reached him first. Canavan said, "It's all right. Drag him back to the fire."

To Neisha he said, "Come on," and walked back to the fire himself with her following a pace behind. He said, "I put my hand down on a prickly pear. Will you help me pull out the spines?"

In the flickering firelight, he looked at her face. It was bruised from Healey's fists, but there was a twinkling in her eyes and the faintest of smiles upon her lips.

Her wry and mocking amusement was directed at them both. She had been foolish in going off alone. Jason had been equally foolish tackling Healey with his fists.

She sat down beside the fire and took his hand and patiently began to remove the cactus spines. The two bounty hunters dragged Healey into camp and immediately put the manacles on him. One of them looked at Neisha's face and growled at Canavan. "You'd better let us take him back. He'll kill her if you don't."

EIGHT

IN THE MORNING, CANAVAN'S HAND WAS SWOLLEN and painful. His head ached from the blow Healey had delivered with the fisted rock. His muscles were stiff and sore. But he could see that Healey was equally uncomfortable. The man scowled at him. He made a taunting obscene gesture at Neisha that she did not see. Canavan walked angrily toward him.

He stood looking down at Healey furiously, "Hanging's too good for you. You ought to be turned over to the Indians. They've got ways of killing a man that take a long, long time."

Healey looked up. His eyes hated Canavan silently for a moment before he said, "I won't hang. I'll outlive you and I'll have that squaw before I'm through."

Canavan wanted to hit him. But he couldn't. Not with Healey manacled. He turned away.

MacCorkindale and Hurley were squatting beside a small fire. Canavan approached. MacCorkindale asked, "How far are we behind those Indians?"

"Fifteen miles."

"Then we could catch them if we wanted to?"

Canavan nodded. "I suppose we could, but it wouldn't do any good. They still outnumber us four to one."

"It's my duty to engage them. And to rescue Edith Thorne."

"They'll kill her if we attack."

"You can't be sure of that. Are you sure you want her rescued, Mr. Canavan?"

"What do you mean by that?"

"Only that it would simplify things for you if the Apaches did kill Edith Thorne."

Canavan said, "Lieutenant, you may feel guilty because of the way they captured her, but don't plan on using me to ease your conscience for you."

Sergeant Hurley glared at Canavan, but after a moment the Lieutenant said, "I guess I deserved that,

Mr. Canavan."

In a less hostile tone, Canavan said, "You said there was a detachment out of Fort Chiricahua looking for these renegades. Sooner or later, this bunch is going to have to join up with Chavo's outfit and when that happens, we'll probably run into the detachment from the fort. We'll outnumber the Indians for a change."

"That will be too late for me."

"Losing what's left of us won't help you, Lieutenant. And that's what would happen if you attacked them now."

"Won't she be in worse danger if the Apaches holding her are attacked by a larger force?"

Canavan nodded, frowning. "But I don't see any other way."

"What if we were to slip into the Apache camp by night and rescue her?"

Canavan stared at him unbelievingly. "You can't be serious."

"But I am serious. You say we don't dare attack the Indians now and you say we don't dare attack them after we meet up with the main command. What choice does that leave us, Mr. Canavan?"

Canavan growled, "You must be out of your mind." He turned away, went to his horse, saddled him and then saddled Neisha's horse. Neisha killed her fire and tied her cooking utensils on behind her saddle. She mounted and sat waiting patiently.

MacCorkindale and Hurley swiftly saddled their own horses. Hurley watched while the bounty hunters readied their own and Healey's mounts. Pixler boosted Healey into his saddle after manacling his hands behind his back. Canavan led out. The bounty hunters and Healey followed. MacCorkindale and Hurley brought up the rear.

Canavan frowned to himself as he followed the Apache trail into the shimmering desert to the south. He had told MacCorkindale it would be foolish to attack the Apaches now. He had told him it would be equally foolish to attack them later, after joining up with the troops from Fort Chiricahua. Then what *did* he intend to do? Was he just following the renegades as a means of salving his conscience? Was the lieutenant right in accusing him of wanting Edith dead?

He shook his head. He didn't believe that. But if he didn't want her dead, how did he propose to rescue her?

At first, MacCorkindale's suggestion that they slip into the Apache camp by night had seemed too foolhardy to be worthy of consideration. Now he began to consider it.

Molocek and Pixler wouldn't help. They'd simply refuse to go and he couldn't blame them if they did. Edith Thorne meant nothing to them. They were along on this expedition only because they were being forced. Nor would Healey be of any help.

That left MacCorkindale and his sergeant. It left Neisha and himself. But if MacCorkindale and Hurley both came along, the two bounty hunters would simply take Healey and depart. So Hurley would have to stay behind to keep an eye on them.

Three then. MacCorkindale, Neisha and himself. Three, to slip into the camp of twenty or more Apaches and snatch a captive out from under their noses. He pushed the idea determinedly away from him. It was impossible. Trying it would only get them killed. He thought reluctantly of Edith, being held by the renegades. He thought of the terror she must be experiencing, having seen the Flores family killed,

59

waiting for the time when they would murder her.

They were crossing relatively level desert now. The mountains were only a faint line against the horizon in the east. There were fewer saguaros here, and less vegetation of other varieties. The heat increased steadily as the sun rose higher in the sky.

Canavan continued to frown as he rode along. He kept his eyes on the Apache trail, beckoning from ahead, but his thoughts stayed with the suggestion MacCorkindale had made. Maybe it was possible. It was worth trying, he admitted reluctantly. They could slip up on the Apache camp by night. They might be able to spot Edith Thorne by the light of the fires. Once they had located her, they might be able to go in silently and rescue her. Surprise would be on their side. The Apaches had no idea they were being followed. They had no idea there were any white men within a hundred miles.

If it was going to be tried, though, it would have to be tried tonight. They were considerably less than a hundred miles from the Mexican border. Tomorrow the Apaches they were following might join the main band, and then rescue would be totally impossible.

Having accepted the idea of trying to rescue Edith Thorne, Canavan urged his horse to a slightly faster pace, wanting to close the distance separating them from the Indians to less than ten miles before darkness forced a stop.

The hours dragged. At nightfall, Canavan guessed they must be no more than fifty or sixty miles from the border of Mexico. He halted his horse and swung to the ground. He waited until MacCorkindale reached him and then he said, "We'll try it, Lieutenant. It's stupid, but I guess it's the only chance we've got. Tomorrow night, they could be in Mexico and our chance of rescuing Edith Thorne will be gone for good."

MacCorkindale looked at Healey and the bounty hunters. "What about them?"

"They'll have to stay here. Your sergeant will also have to stay behind to keep an eye on them."

MacCorkindale beckoned Sergeant Hurley. "We're going to overtake the Indians. We're going to try slipping into their camp and rescuing Miss Thorne. You're to stay and watch Healey and the two bounty hunters until we get back."

Hurley saluted and said, "Yes, Sir," but there was a worried frown upon his face. MacCorkindale said, "If we don't get back by dawn, release Healey into the custody of the two bounty hunters and try to make it back to Fort Chiricahua by yourself."

"Why can't I go with you, Sir? An extra man might make the difference."

"Because if you come along the bounty hunters will take Healey and go back to Yuma and that's the last we'll see of them."

Hurley nodded grudgingly. Canavan spoke briefly to Neisha and rode away into the gray light of dusk. Neisha followed and MacCorkindale brought up the rear. Pixler and Molocek crossed to Hurley and questioned him about where they were going. Hurley answered curtly, then began to build a fire.

Canavan followed the Apache trail for as long as possible. When he could no longer see it from his horse, he dismounted and walked. When be could no longer see it in walking, he called to Neisha, who took the lead, bending low so that she could see the trail.

When even Neisha could no longer see, Canavan stopped. He knew the direction of the trail. It had not deviated for more than a dozen miles. He said, "There may be sentries out. I'll go ahead. You two stay back as far as you can. If you lose sight of me, close up. If I'm attacked, turn around and head back to camp as fast as you can go. Is that understood?"

Neither Neisha nor MacCorkindale replied. Canavan said, "Lieutenant, she may not want to go. You may have to take her back by force."

"All right."

"I can count on you?"

MacCorkindale hesitated only briefly. Then he said, "You can count on me."

"Let's go then." Canavan led off. The others waited until he was nearly out of sight in the darkness. Then they followed, Neisha on silent feet, MacCorkindale not so silently.

Canavan traveled several miles before he stopped. He had lost the trail completely now. Neisha caught up, followed immediately by MacCorkindale. Canavan stared at the stars. He guessed it was nearly eleven o'clock. Another five or six miles probably separated them from the Apache camp, but he could not be sure of that. The renegades might have stopped sooner than usual or they might have traveled later than usual. The one thing Canavan did not want to do was blunder into the Apache camp before he knew that it was there.

He said, "Take my horse, Neisha. I can be quieter afoot."

She silently took the reins. Canavan looked at her. She was outwardly submissive as her Indian training had taught her to be. Inside she had feelings like any other woman. He put his arms around her for a moment and held her close to him. There was much he wanted to tell her but this was not the time. Not like this. Not with

62

Lieutenant MacCorkindale listening. She was warm and she was trembling. She was afraid for him but she also probably resented him risking his life for the kidnapped white woman. And she must be afraid of what would happen if he was successful in rescuing Edith Thorne.

He wanted to tell her that he would not marry Edith Thorne, that he would not send her back to the reservation. He opened his mouth to tell her, then closed it again. He thought, "Not now. Not yet," and he wondered at himself. Was he holding back because he was in doubt?

Frowning, he released her. On silent feet he moved away, growing ever more cautious now because he knew the Apache camp was close. At frequent intervals he stopped and stood motionless, listening. Sometimes he would hear Neisha and MacCorkindale coming on behind. But he heard nothing from ahead.

Midnight passed and he still had not encountered the Indian camp. He began to wonder with a kind of quiet panic if he could have passed it in the dark. Then, suddenly, he topped a low rise of ground and heard horses fidgeting ahead of him

He stopped instantly and waited for Neisha and MacCorkindale to catch up. When they had, he whispered softly. "You two move back a ways and wait. I'll go on and take a look."

He remained still until they had retreated, until he could no longer hear the sounds of their horses' hoofs. Then he eased slowly forward, testing each footstep before he put his weight on it, taking care that he touched no brush, no cactus that might make a scratching sound against his clothes.

Suddenly, he heard a man's deep voice. He could tell that the words were in the Apache tongue but he

63

couldn't make them out. He froze, then went on, even more cautiously than before. He was a shadow now, making no more noise than any shadow moving across the desert floor.

Some rocks loomed up ahead. He crouched behind them and stared at the scene below. There were several small fires burning. Most of them had died to glowing beds of coals, but two burned brightly. Several of the Apaches were sleeping, their shapes lumped and indistinct against the ground. A few moved around or sat cross-legged silently staring into the flames. Straining to see, Canavan searched for Edith but she was nowhere in sight. He eased back, even more careful than before. Only when he had put a full three hundred yards between himself and his former vantage point did he dare move more rapidly.

He encountered Neisha and MacCorkindale a quarter mile back. Quickly he told MacCorkindale what he had seen. "I think we ought to tie the horses and go on afoot. The Indians are still stirring around and we can't do a thing until they settle down. While we're waiting, though, maybe we can spot Edith Thorne." Leading the others, he headed back toward the Apache camp.

NINE

HAVING ONCE MORE REACHED THE ROCKS FROM WHICH he had earlier observed the Apache camp, Canavan halted. He knelt down. MacCorkindale squatted on his right, Neisha on his left.

Fewer of the Apaches were now moving around. Canavan counted only three. In addition, he knew one of the younger ones would be with the horse herd, bunched beyond the camp.

MacCorkindale whispered, "I don't see Miss Thorne."

"I didn't see her a while ago."

"Maybe she's asleep."

"Not likely. It would be more likely that they'd be working her. Maybe she's out gathering firewood."

"Lord, if we only knew where!"

"We don't. And we can't go blundering around in the dark. The Apaches may not know we're here, but I'd bet anything they've got sentries out."

A figure suddenly appeared near one of the fires and put down an armload of sticks. It was Edith Thorne. Canavan heard MacCorkindale release a long, slow sigh. He glanced at Neisha, but there was insufficient light to read the expression on her face.

Canavan returned his glance to Edith Thorne. He had not seen her for more than a year, and at this distance it would have been difficult to recognize anyone. But even up close he doubted if he'd now recognize Edith Thorne. She wore no hat and her hair was matted and uncombed. Her clothes were filthy and torn in a dozen places. She limped as though both feet were very sore. He knew what the condition of her face would be. Without the protection of a hat, she'd be blistered and raw from the merciless rays of the Arizona sun. He felt an immediate pity for her. However indirectly, her condition was as much his fault as it was MacCorkindale's. She had come here only because of him.

Now he noticed that one of the Apache braves who was still awake turned his head and was speaking to her. She halted, face turned toward him, obviously not understanding what he said. He got up, approached her

65

and spoke again. The distance was too great to hear his words, but it was plain enough that he had ordered her to do something and that she still had not understood. She shrank away as he approached, and he struck her hard enough to knock her down. He spoke again, and pointed, and Edith got up and hurried out of the circle of firelight.

Canavan had stiffened when the Indian struck her. MacCorkindale had uttered a low-voiced curse. The lieutenant now said, "Let's go get her, Mr. Canavan. From the looks of her, she isn't going to last."

Canavan said, "You two stay here. Three of us haven't a chance of getting in there without being heard or seen. I'll go in, but before I do, I want one thing understood, Lieutenant. I'm on my own. If I'm caught, that's my tough luck. You're to take Neisha and go back to Fort Chiricahua."

"I won't do that!"

"Then let's get started back right now. It's suicide for the three of us to try going in together. It would be suicide if you were to start a battle trying to save my hide. The only way there's a chance is if I go in alone. And I'm not so sure that isn't suicide. Suppose I do get her away? You don't think they'll take it lying down, do you? They'll backtrack us and jump us anyway."

"Maybe not. Maybe they're close enough to Mexico so they figure they don't need Miss Thorne as a hostage any more."

"Maybe. And they won't know how big a force is following. They might not want to risk finding out. That's the only reason I'm willing to chance going into their camp."

He turned to look down into Neisha's face. He said, "If I don't get back—" He stopped, groped a moment for words and then went on, "You will not have to go back to the reservation unless you want to go. You can stay on the ranch. The cattle will be yours."

She did not speak. She didn't have to speak for him to know her thoughts. She cared nothing for the ranch, cared nothing for the cattle that meant so much to him. He was what she cared about and without him she would as soon return to the reservation for good.

He felt an odd sort of helplessness. He felt a kind of guilt as well. But he salved the guilt by thinking that she was no worse off for having lived with him as his wife. At least she hadn't had a child.

He took her face in his hands, stooped and kissed her on the mouth. She was Apache. She was supposed to be impassive and not show her feelings, but suddenly she uttered a sob and threw her arms around his neck. She buried her face in his shirt.

He held her thus for a moment. Then he felt her stiffen and knew it was time to let her go. She moved away a step or two. For an instant he felt a sense of loss. He looked at MacCorkindale. "I have your word?"

"You have my word."

Canavan moved away immediately, walking slowly and silently, testing each step before putting his weight fully down. His ears were tuned to each small sound. His eyes probed the darkness on each side of him and straight ahead.

He made a slow half circle of the camp. It was possible that he was wrong about their having sentries out but he didn't intend to count on it. On the far side of camp he cut between it and the horse herd. He stopped, trying to penetrate the darkness with his glance, hoping with quiet desperation that he would see Edith Thorne. If he had to go all the way into the Apache camp for her, he'd have less chance of getting safely out again.

He did not see her and went on. The horse herd was now behind. The Apache camp was on his left. And suddenly, straight ahead of him, he saw Edith Thorne.

She was kneeling beside the carcass of a horse, trying to cut chunks of meat out of a hindquarter from which the hide had been partially removed. Canavan stopped, uneasy, aware that if he spoke to her or called her name she might become hysterical and give him away.

Frozen, he watched her work. She made but a dim figure in the light from the stars, in the small amount of light cast this far by the fires in the Apache camp. Canavan's mouth thinned. Tomorrow the Apaches would leave most of the horse's carcass behind but they would have eaten their fill and would carry enough meat with them to last for several days. This was one reason, he thought, why they were able to thwart the cavalry so easily. Essentially foot travelers, they used horses but they had no love for them. They rode them until they dropped and then they used their carcasses for food.

Carefully Canavan approached the girl. A dozen yards away he said softly, "Edith. It's Jason Canavan. Don't make a sound and stay right where you are. I've come to take you away."

She froze. She made no sound. For the briefest instant he thought she would remain silent. Then, as he took a step toward her, her self-control suddenly disappeared. With a cry of hysteria that was almost a scream she left the horse carcass and ran. She hadn't seen him but she had heard his voice. She ran toward the place from where the sound had come.

Canavan moved toward her, prepared to scoop her up in his arms and make a run for it. Now that she had screamed, it was all that was left for him to do. But suddenly, beyond her, the shape of a running Apache brave came into sight, carbine in one hand, knife in the other.

Canavan veered aside. Edith Thorne went past, still searching for him, not seeing him. She ran straight into the Apache camp and stopped, staring around in bewilderment.

Canavan glanced behind. The three Apaches who were awake had come to their feet and were now staring at their white captive as if trying to understand what had made her cry out so unexpectedly. In a matter of minutes they'd come to investigate, particularly if they heard the sounds of a scuffle here.

The sentry had seen him, and had now veered toward him. Canavan swung right, running hard, putting the camp and Edith Thorne behind. His chance to rescue her was gone. He cursed softly beneath his breath as he ran. If she hadn't lost control—If she had remained still—But she hadn't and now it was too late.

The sentry pursued him eagerly. Canavan wondered why he did not cry out for the others. Then he understood. This was a young brave who wanted to kill him single-handedly. He wanted all the glory for himself.

Canavan could hear his footsteps a few yards behind. He kept going, not trying to get away but only to put enough distance between himself and the Apache camp so that their fight would not be heard. He had to kill the sentry to buy time for Neisha and MacCorkindale and himself. And besides, he wanted to. For Sam Flores and his family.

Not until he had put five hundred yards between himself and the fires did he halt and whirl. He still could not afford a gunshot. That could be heard even at a distance of more than a quarter mile. So it would have to be hand to hand and the first thing he had to do was get the Apache's rifle away from him.

The man swiftly closed the distance separating them. He must have been surprised that Canavan chose to turn and fight. Or perhaps he understood, too late, that Caravan had only lured him away from his companions so that they could fight it out undisturbed.

He brought his rifle up, but he got no chance to fire it. Canavan plunged toward him, striking him bodily and seizing the rifle at contact. The wiry young brave was strong, but so was Canavan. He wrenched the rifle from the Indian and flung it into the desert emptiness. He had used two hands doing so. He had used both hands knowing that one of the Apache's hands held a knife. That had been the risk and now the knife raked his thigh, cutting deep and drawing a flood of blood. But with both hands free, he groped for and seized the Indian's knife arm, shifting his grip swiftly and surely to the man's wrist.

They rolled through a clump of prickly pear and the Apache let out a grunt of pain. Canavan felt the spines penetrate his shirt and back and then he too had rolled on past.

Blood drenched his thigh, warm and frightening. He wondered how deep the cut had been and how swiftly he was losing blood. He knew he had to get this over quickly or he might weaken enough from loss of blood so that the Apache could overcome him.

He shifted the grip of one of his hands to the Indian's elbow. Then, flat on his back, he raised a knee, at the same time bringing the Indian's arm down violently.

He felt the contact of the Indian's arm against his rising knee. He heard the unmistakable snapping sound of the bone as it broke. And he heard the Indian's indrawn breath . . .

The knife dropped from the Indian's unfeeling fingers. Canavan wasted no time groping for it. His hands sought and found the Apache's throat.

The Indian was thrashing violently now, trying to throw him off, trying to break free. His throat made strange, gurgling sounds as he attempted, too late, to call for help. His knees raised and slammed into Canavan's groin and belly, and his good hand, fingers outstretched, clawed at Canavan's face, seeking to gouge out his eyes.

Canavan could defend himself only by turning his head, and by turning it back as the Indian's questing fingers sought his eye sockets again and again. Those raking fingers found one of his eyes, and dug in deep. Pain shot through Canavan's head like a knife. Every instinct screamed at him to release the Apache's throat and save his eye, but he resisted it and only tightened his hands more determinedly. Convulsively he heaved his body into an arc, then whipped it straight again. The Indian's hand was torn away, but the pain remained, stabbing repeatedly through Canavan's brain.

Had the Indian succeeded in blinding him? The thought so infuriated him that he gave one last surge of strength to his hands. The Indian had now been without air for several minutes. His struggles weakened. His hand stopped seeking Canavan's eyes. His feet and knees stopped trying to jab into Canavan's belly and groin.

Canavan held on until the Indian went limp, and even after that. He held on until he was certain the Apache brave was dead, until there was no longer movement in the man's chest. He released his grip then and rolled away, panting with exertion and too weak to rise. He listened, and raised a fearful hand to his burning, streaming eye and felt tears, or blood, or both pouring from it. But the eyeball itself was still in its socket. The Indian had failed.

Next, Canavan put a hand to his thigh. He could feel the cut, perhaps three inches long, perhaps half an inch deep. It ran lengthwise of his leg, so it was doubtful if any muscles or tendons had been cut. But his whole leg was drenched with blood and he was growing weaker. He got up, stood still long enough to get his bearings, then limped swiftly toward the place he had left Neisha and Lieutenant MacCorkindale.

They had tried to save Edith Thorne and they had failed. To make matters worse when the Apaches found the strangled brave they would backtrack and find the place where MacCorkindale, Neisha and Canavan had lain and watched their camp. They would probably assume the three were simply scouting for a larger force. If so, they would go on toward Mexico, travelling faster than before.

In any case, Edith Thorne was lost. If they didn't kill her, one of the braves would probably take her as his wife. It might be years before they brought her back from Mexico.

Canavan growled a savage, helpless curse.

TEN

NEISHA BOUND UP CANAVAN'S STREAMING THIGH WITH strips torn from her petticoat. Without knowing the condition of his eye, he hurriedly led them away from the Indians' camp. He didn't know how far the Apaches

72

would backtrack them, but he hoped it would not be for long.

Dawn showed them no one following. No column of dust rose out of the desert to the south. Canavan released a long sigh of relief. He looked at Neisha, tears still welling from his injured eye. "My eye. Is it all right?"

She rode close and when he stopped, peered into the injured eye. He asked, "Is it bleeding?"

"No. But it is very red."

He nodded. "That's all right. I can see, so I guess there's no harm done."

MacCorkindale took Neisha's place beside Canavan as she fell back. "What are we going to do now? What *can* we do?"

Canavan shrugged. "We can get your sergeant, the two bounty hunters, and Healey and keep on following."

"What good is that? They still outnumber us. Only now they're on their guard."

Canavan asked, "Have you got any better ideas?"

The lieutenant shook his head.

"Then that's what we'll do. Maybe we'll be lucky enough to run into the troops from Fort Chiricahua."

They traveled the entire ten miles between the Apache camp and their own without encountering Sergeant Hurley, the bounty hunters, or their prisoner.

When they reached the camp, it was deserted. Even though he had half expected it, Canavan uttered a sour curse. His wound and the pain in his eye had made him irritable. Now he realized they would have to trail the bounty hunters who must have overcome Sergeant Hurley, disarmed him and headed for Yuma with their prisoners. Hurley would be tracking.

Angrily, Canavan circled the camp. He picked up the

trail without difficulty and beckoned to the others to follow him.

His irritability increased as he rode now toward the west. Every mile they followed the bounty hunters along this trail put them a mile farther away from the Apaches who had kidnapped Edith Thorne and murdered the Flores family. His hope of being able to rescue her began to fade. Damn! If she hadn't panicked last night, she'd be with them now. They'd be safe, because the Indians wouldn't have risked following and tangling with a larger force.

MacCorkindale was as glum as Canavan. He rode behind Neisha, his head sunk forward dispiritedly. He hadn't had a shave for days and his face and clothes were covered with a fine yellow dust.

Canavan's leg throbbed steadily. Looking down, he saw that blood had seeped through both the heavy bandage and through his dusty trouser leg. He felt dizzy. His head began to ache savagely, he supposed from the pressure the Indian had put upon his eyeball trying to gouge it out.

He glanced around at Neisha, wondering for the first time what she thought of what was happening. If he had expected to see gloating or triumph in her expression, he was disappointed. She gazed steadily at him. He could see that she had forgotten Edith Thorne. There was only worried concern for him in her eyes.

He was suddenly ashamed for the worry he was causing her. He knew she was afraid that if he managed to get Edith away from the Indians, he would marry her. He owed it to Neisha to reassure her, but that was something he could not yet do. He thought he wanted Neisha. He thought he would be able to send Edith Thorne away if and when they managed to rescue her.

74

But he was not completely sure and he would not be sure until Edith Thorne was free again.

Alternately he trotted and walked his horse. There had been neither dew nor wind, and it was difficult to tell with any certainty how old the trail was that they were following. But at last, straight ahead and no more than a couple of miles away, he spotted a lift of dust and shortly there after saw the distant figure of a man and horse. Hurley, he thought probably little more than a rifle shot behind the bounty hunters and their prisoner.

In midmorning, they caught up with Hurley, who had stopped to wait for them. He was sitting in the shade cast by a giant saguaro. He stood up and saluted the Lieutenant sheepishly as the three approached. "They sneaked up behind me, Sir, and took my gun. They got their own guns out of my saddlebags. I guess I just haven't got any good excuse." He looked at the faces of the three, one by one. He noted the redness of Canavan's eye and the blood on his thigh. "Couldn't get Miss Thorne away from them?"

Canavan shook his head.

"Looks like you tangled with one of them redskinned renegades."

Canavan nodded again. "How far are those two bounty hunters ahead of you?"

"Half a mile. They shot at me a couple of times, trying to make me stop, but they gave up when they saw I wasn't goin' to."

MacCorkindale said, "All right, let's go. Canavan, you stay here and rest. Hurley and I can bring them back."

Canavan nodded. He was feeling weaker all the time, and dizzier. He dismounted and sat down in the shade where Hurley had been sitting when they arrived.

75

MacCorkindale and Hurley rode away, the sergeant now carrying Canavan's rifle to replace the one the bounty hunters had taken away from him.

Canavan lay back on the ground and closed his eyes. His leg throbbed and the injured eye sent knives of pain stabbing through his head. Neisha brought a water-soaked cloth and laid it over his eyes. He reached out and took her hand. And then, in spite of the heat, in spite of his pain, he went to sleep.

MacCorkindale rode his horse at a steady trot. Within fifteen minutes he spotted the bounty hunters and Healey dead ahead. They had been riding in a dry wash, but now as they came out of it, they turned to look behind. MacCorkindale drew his revolver and fired a single warning shot above their heads.

They did not stop. Instead, they urged their horses on at a trot. MacCorkindale dug his spurs into his own mount's side and the animal broke into a reluctant lope. His neck was already dark with sweat.

The bounty hunters also broke into a lope. Healey's horse, being led by Molocek, was slowing them by pulling against the reins. MacCorkindale dug spurs into his horse's sides again, forcing a little more speed from him. He began to overtake the fugitives.

Soon, he thought, they'd realize that it was only a matter of time before he and Sergeant Hurley caught up with them. When they did, they'd stop and probably put up a fight. But would they risk killing to get away? He shook his head almost imperceptibly at the thought. He couldn't be sure but he didn't intend to give them a chance to kill either him or Sergeant Hurley if it could be helped.

The three fugitives descended, sliding, into another

dry wash, raising a cloud of dust. Instantly, MacCorkindale waved Sergeant Hurley toward the left, while he veered sharply to the right.

MacCorkindale's temper was, by now, even shorter than Canavan's. His shoulder had a dull, constant ache that put his nerves on edge. He was dead tired and he was discouraged at their failure to get Edith Thorne away from the Apache camp last night. To compound his frustration, they'd had to give up the pursuit of the Apaches and take a time-consuming side trail after these defecting bounty hunters because without them they had just as well not bother following the Apache band at all.

He reached the lip of the wash and spurred his horse to force him over the steep precipice. The animal hesitated, then went over, half sliding, half jumping. MacCorkindale caught a quick glimpse of the two bounty hunters and Healey. They had dismounted. Healey crouched on the far side of the wash, swiping a hand at a bleeding nose and glaring at the bounty hunters' backs. Molocek and Pixler were scrambling up the near side of the wash to ambush the lieutenant and sergeant when they got in easy range.

MacCorkindale yelled, "Hold it right there, you two! You're covered!"

The pair who were off balance, using both hands and feet to get up the sloping side of the wash, suddenly froze. In that instant, MacCorkindale's horse lost his footing and went to his knees, catapulting the lieutenant forward. He held onto his gun, but by the time he had recovered and gained his feet, Molocek had the drop on him. Hurley, beyond, had dismounted. He had Canavan's rifle in his hands, but was afraid to use it as long as the bounty hunters had the drop on MacCorkindale.

MacCorkindale said evenly, "Sergeant, if they do not drop their guns by the time I count to three, you are to shoot to kill. Do you understand?"

Hurley's eyes were worried, but he said, "Yes, Sir!"

MacCorkindale said, "One."

Molocek scowled. "You dumb bastard, are you stupid? We got guns on you. You tell that sergeant to drop his gun or by God you're dead!"

MacCorkindale said, "Two."

Molocek's face assumed an expression of furious desperation. For an instant MacCorkindale thought he would really shoot. He tried to make his expression confident as he looked Molocek straight in the eye. Pixler opened his mouth to say something just as MacCorkindale opened his for the final count.

Molocek yelled, "All right! All right! Tell him not to shoot!" He threw his gun into the bottom of the wash. Pixler lost no time in following suit.

Molocek growled, "Crazy bastards! There ain't an ounce of brains in the lot of you! What's so damn important about that woman anyway that we all got to risk our necks to get her loose?"

MacCorkindale walked to the rifles and picked them up. He said, "I'll take your revolvers too."

"You ain't goin' to get them, you son of a bitch! I ain't goin' around unarmed where there's Apaches runnin' loose. Besides, there's Healey. He's killed before an' he will again if he gets the chance."

MacCorkindale said, "Sergeant."

Molocek glanced at the sergeant, then back at MacCorkindale. Sullenly he threw his revolver into the bottom of the wash. Pixler did likewise. MacCorkindale picked up both guns.

He carried them to Sergeant Hurley. "Tie these on

your saddle, sergeant. Then let's get started back."

He turned and looked at the bounty hunters. He glanced quickly at Healey and back again. "The three of you are going with us and you're going to help whether you like it or not."

"By God, you've got no authority—"

MacCorkindale interrupted, "The sergeant is holding my authority. Now shut up and get mounted. We've lost enough time today as is."

He walked to his horse and swung up. He watched the two bounty hunters mount. Healey climbed on his horse and sullenly followed Hurley out of the wash. Molocek and Pixler followed. MacCorkindale brought up the rear, his angry irritability only slightly mollified.

ELEVEN

LEM HEALEY RODE BEHIND SERGEANT HURLEY, scowling, but feeling a vast relief. He was deathly afraid of Molocek and Pixler, because he knew neither of them cared whether they delivered him to Yuma Prison alive or dead. A severed leg with the plain, scabbed marks of the manacles would get them the reward as quickly as would his whole body. He further knew that to the bounty hunters he was not a human being at all, but just a savage animal with a price on his head. They knew he had killed repeatedly. They knew he would kill again if he wasn't hanged.

But now he had a reprieve. He and the bounty hunters had been caught. They would once more take the Apaches' trail, and a lot could happen in the next few days. Molocek and Pixler might be killed. Canavan and the two troopers also might be killed. He might even get that pretty Apache squaw . . .

He stared thoughtfully at Hurley's brawny back, at the sergeant's beet-red neck. He admitted that he didn't dare count on the Apaches to get rid of his captors for him. It wasn't even certain that they'd be able to catch up with the renegades. He would have to do something himself about getting loose. But what was the good of that? Even if he managed to escape, Molocek and Pixler would catch up with him. The only way he'd get clear away was if they were dead.

Behind him, Molocek and Pixler began to bicker sourly about who was to blame for getting caught. Irritated, MacCorkindale was telling them both to shut their mouths. It was plain that the lieutenant's shoulder was festering, and the sergeant's narrowed, pain-filled eyes gave away the discomfort of his head wound. Molocek and Pixler were furious over being caught and made to turn around and chase the Apache renegades. It ought to be easy to pit one against the other if it was done skillfully. Running these ideas through his mind, Healey began to grin.

He turned his head and looked at Lieutenant MacCorkindale. The lieutenant's face occasionally twisted with pain each time his horse jolted him. Healey said, "Lieutenant, what does the army do to an officer who loses four of his men and has a woman he's escorting captured by the Indians? Are they satisfied to bust him, or do they kick him out of the service too?"

Immediately ahead, Sergeant Hurley turned in his saddle furiously. "Shut yer dirty mouth, ye bastard, or I'll shut it with me fist." Hurley never reverted to his brogue except under the most stressing of circumstances.

MacCorkindale, whose face was almost as red as the

sergeant's neck, said, "Never mind, Sergeant."

Healey persisted, "What *do* they do, Lieutenant? Do they ever send a man like that to an army prison for what he's done? Looks to me like it's murder just as sure as if he put a gun to them troopers' heads himself."

Molocek and Pixler had stopped bickering. They glanced at Healey, then turned their heads to look at the Lieutenant's face. Molocek asked, "How about it, Lieutenant? You did lose four men and you lost that woman to the Indians. It *was* your fault, wasn't it? If you'd been farther out on the desert floor where they couldn't have ambushed you—"

Hurley snarled, "Them red bastards kin ambush ye anywhere. They kin hide where there ain't nothin' to hide behind."

Healey persisted, "But you were in a hurry, weren't you, MacCorkindale? You didn't like bein' sent to escort a woman when the whole garrison was goin' after the Indians. You were trying to get her to Canavan's and get away in time to catch up with the rest of the troops."

MacCorkindale said, "I suppose I was."

Hurley said, "Lieutenant, don't give the son of a bitch that much satisfaction, Sir. What right has a dirty murderer like him got to criticize a fine man like you?"

Healey turned his head to the front again and looked Hurley squarely in the eye. "Whose side are you on, Sergeant? Wasn't them four troopers friends of yours? Are you goin' to cover up the lieutenant's stupidity for him? What if you was to have to write the letters to them four troopers' families? What would you tell their families about how they died?"

MacCorkindale said, "Healey, shut your mouth. You're just trying to stir up trouble and I'm not going to

81

let you get away with it. If you want to make any accusations, save them for when we get back to the fort."

"Maybe we ain't goin' to get back to the fort. There's twenty Apache bucks ahead of us. There's more somewhere ahead of them. What if our twenty was to join up with the rest? You think any of us would get back alive?" He looked at Pixler and Molocek. "You can't spend any bounty money if you're dead."

Molocek said, "Shut up, Healey."

"Sure, I'll shut up. But if the two of you got any sense, you'll see that you're bein' used. That lieutenant don't give a damn about you. He don't give a damn about nobody but himself. He had four troopers an' he got them killed by the same Indians we been following. You want to jump the Indians with a man like that in command?"

Hurley stopped. He reined close to Healey's horse and swung a savage right that missed. Healey grinned mockingly. Hurley's face got redder than before. MacCorkindale said sharply, "Sergeant, that's enough!"

"Yes, Sir." Hurley glared a moment, then kicked his horse into motion again.

Healey knew he had done enough for now. Grinning slightly, he let his head loll forward. He had knotted the reins and they now lay looped over his saddle horn. He didn't need to guide his horse. He didn't need to trail or watch the desert or be on guard. He closed his eyes. It was a good time to get a little sleep, even if it only consisted of dozing while he rode. The time might come when it would be important for him to be rested and able to stay awake. His life might depend on it.

Besides, he had said enough to get their minds to chewing on the things he'd said. Hurley would begin to doubt his lieutenant and to wonder if his loyalties did not properly belong with the four troopers the Apache renegades had killed.

MacCorkindale, already questioning his own conduct, would feel even guiltier than before—now that it had all been put into words that everyone had heard.

And the bounty hunters were already resentful at being forced to chase the Apache renegades when all they wanted to do was return their prisoner to Yuma and collect the reward. Knowing they were being used to help correct the lieutenant's mistake wouldn't help their dispositions much. They'd probably try to get away again. There might be gunplay when they did. There had almost been gunplay a while ago in the bottom of that wash. There would have been except that Molocek and Pixler had recognized that when the lieutenant ordered Sergeant Hurley to shoot, he meant his order to be obeyed. But what if their judgment had been impaired? What if they had called the lieutenant's bluff?

Healey dozed, awakened, and dozed again. The desert heat was constant and brutal, but it was something that bothered him very little now. If you could endure the terrible heat of the exercise yard at Yuma, you could endure anything.

Canavan, who was still sleeping when they reached the place where they had left him, awakened as they approached. Healey leered at Neisha, knowing Canavan was watching him. Canavan got up and limped painfully to his horse. He mounted, waited briefly while Neisha mounted, then led out toward the east.

He was scowling and Healey grinned to himself. He had maneuvered it so that he was immediately behind the Indian girl. Molocek and Pixler rode behind him, followed by Hurley and MacCorkindale. He kept his

83

steady, burning glance on Neisha's back and was rewarded when a dull flush crept up into her neck.

Canavan turned his head and glared straight into Healey's eyes. His voice was soft but it was venomous. "You son of a bitch, take your eyes off her or I'm going to save the hangman in Yuma some trouble."

Neisha protested worriedly, "It is all right. He does not bother me."

"He bothers *me*," growled Canavan.

Healey didn't let the grin fade from his face. He asked, "Why do I bother you, Mr. Canavan? Or is it your conscience that really bothers you?"

"What the hell are you talking about?"

"You say you couldn't get the white woman out of the Apache camp last night, but how do we know that's true? Maybe you didn't want to get her out."

Neisha turned her head and glanced at him confusedly. Healey's grin widened. He said, "Don't let it go to your head, girlie. It ain't you that Canavan's worried about. He's worried about his stinking hide and about his ranch and cattle back there on Furnace Creek. Without you, he knows damn well that he wouldn't last a week. Chavo's young bucks would feed him to the ants."

Neisha glanced back at Canavan. Healey turned in his saddle and looked at Lieutenant MacCorkindale. "You got the wrong man trailing for you, Lieutenant, if you want to get that woman back and clear yourself with your superiors. He ain't about to get her back, unless it's dead."

MacCorkindale said, "Oh shut up, for Christ's sake! Haven't we got enough trouble without stirring up some more?" But he was looking at Canavan as he spoke, a fleeting question in his eyes.

Healey glanced at Neisha, a triumphant grin now broader on his face. It was working, he thought. It was working and would go on working if he had sense enough not to push it too far.

But he still wanted to plant some doubts in Neisha's mind. He said, "You're a pretty squaw and I guess you can keep Canavan warm nights as well as any woman could, but you don't think for a minute he's goin' to keep you around any longer than he has to, do you? You're still a red Indian and if Canavan's like the rest of the settlers in this territory he hates red Indians and especially Apache red Indians. Soon's the Army catches Chavo an' his renegades and puts them away for good, he'll send you packin' to the reservation along with whatever red Indian brats you've got by that time. He'll take this Edith Thorne and marry her and in a couple of months he won't even remember what you look like any more."

In a tone trembling with outrage Canavan said, "Healey, damn you—"

But Healey wasn't finished. He said, "Young squaws are fine, but Canavan knows that when they get older they get fat and ugly. So if I was you, I'd get word to your brother, Chavo. I'd tell him to kill that white woman so's Canavan can't get her back"

Canavan's voice was level and tight with his efforts at self-control. He said, "Neisha, don't listen to anything he says. He's a murderer that will do anything to save his skin. He's trying to get us all to distrust each other so that he'll have a better chance to get away."

Neisha looked at him, then back at Healey, then back at Canavan again. There was a puzzled frown upon her forehead and a suspicious brightness in her eyes. Canavan said almost pleadingly, "He's taunted me with

85

not wanting Edith back alive because he said I wanted to stay with you. He's taunted you by telling you I'll send you back to the reservation and marry her. Don't let him bother you. I—"

Healey laughed aloud. "What were you goin' to tell her, Canavan? That you love her and want to marry her? Do you think that will convince her now?"

Canavan looked at Molocek. "If you want him to stay alive, you'd better muzzle him."

Molocek said, "Shut up, Healey or I'll stuff your mouth full of rags."

Healey shrugged. He could afford to be silent now. He had planted his seeds of discord. Now let them grow. He let his head sink forward again and closed his eyes. He dozed again.

The sun made its inexorable journey across the sky. The horses traveled listlessly. Even these men who were accustomed to the heat suffered from it today.

Canavan fumed helplessly for more than an hour after Healey had finished taunting him. He thought about Edith, and wondered how it was possible for her to endure this heat, for her to endure the terror the Apaches must inspire in her. She had seen them kill the Flores family. She had been beaten and forced to work until she dropped.

And for the first time, he began to question himself. Had he really tried to get Edith away from the Apache camp last night? Or had he, by calling out to her, made it a virtual certainty that she would lose control and become hysterical?

He scowled irritably to himself. Maybe he should have gone to her, put his hand over her mouth, and given her a few moments to gain control of herself.

Maybe. But not necessarily. He knew Edith Thorne.

He knew the strength in her. She had endured much and it had not occurred to him that she would lose control. Or had it?

He cursed Healey for making him doubt himself.

TWELVE

CANAVAN HALTED AT SUNDOWN EVEN THOUGH A great deal of distance still remained between where they now were and the place where he had invaded the Indian camp and killed the Apache guard the night before. In reply to MacCorkindale's questioning glance he said, "We're going to have to travel all night if we're ever going to catch up with them. It's hard on the horses, but I don't know what else we can do."

All unsaddled their horses and rubbed their sweating backs. Canavan fanned his horse and Neisha's with his saddle blanket. The others followed suit.

Neisha built a fire and put coffee on for Canavan and herself. Again the bounty hunters and Healey grouped around a second fire and Sergeant Hurley built a third fire for Leiutenant MacCorkindale and himself.

Canavan gave the horses two hours rest, then led out again in early dusk. It was not necessary to follow trail. He could find the place he was looking for in darkness without difficulty. Tomorrow would be different. He would have to go back to trailing the Indians again.

There was no talking among the members of the group. Healey rode with his head lolling forward, apparently half asleep. Molocek and Pixler, after a brief discussion, had decided that one of them could sleep while the other watched. Pixler slept first, dozing in the saddle as Healey was doing, occasionally snapping wide awake whenever he began to topple to one side.

Hurley also dozed, after being instructed to do so by MacCorkindale. MacCorkindale rode behind Pixler so that the bounty hunters couldn't again try breaking free with their prisoner.

Every two hours, Canavan stopped to give the weary horses rest. It was cooler at night, and in this respect at least the trail was easier.

Dawn broke while they still were a couple of miles short of the place where Canavan had slipped into the Apache camp. At sunup they reached it and Canavan read the tracks worriedly, fearing the Indians might have killed Edith Thorne in reprisal for the death of the brave that he had killed. There was no evidence of a grave. The Apaches must have even taken their dead comrade along with them.

In daylight, Canavan noticed the members of the party looking at each other guardedly. He glanced at Healey and surprised a triumphant smile upon his face. Healey was also watching the various members of the group and it was obvious how well his taunts of yesterday were succeeding among them today. They'd had all night to think. They'd obviously decided there had been at least some truth in the things that he had said.

Irritably, Canavan led out again, feeling disgust for the divisions and bickering among the members of this small group. It was obvious that none of them really cared about Edith Thorne. MacCorkindale was only trying to clear himself of a possible charge of negligence. Hurley was obeying orders. The bounty hunters were along only because they were being forced and Neisha probably would prefer it if Edith Thorne was never seen again.

And how about himself? What did he feel toward Edith? Did he really want her rescued from the Indians?

He searched his own thoughts honestly. He finally decided that he did not want Edith Thorne for himself. He did not want to marry her. But that didn't mean he wanted her to be killed or wanted her to remain forever in captivity.

The trail told him that the Apaches were traveling faster than they had been before. They could have no idea how large was the force pursuing them. They probably figured that those pursuing them must be very numerous or else members of that force would not have dared invade their camp.

In this belief lay his only hope of rescuing Edith Thorne. If he could close the distance, it was possible they could surprise the Apaches by night, and trust the darkness to hide the fact they were outnumbered.

All day they remained on the trail, until at dusk, Canavan dismounted and carefully studied the tracks in the last remaining light. The Apaches could not now be more than a few miles ahead. By traveling all night, he and the others had made up the time lost in following the fugitives. But now everyone was near exhaustion and the horses had to have some rest. The border of Mexico was close ahead, probably less than half a day from here . . .

Canavan returned to the group. He looked at MacCorkindale. "If we're going to hit them, it will have to be tonight. From the way they're traveling, I'd guess they think a good-sized force is chasing them. By attacking in the dark, it's just possible we can keep them from finding out how wrong they are."

Molocek stared at him. "You must be out of your mind. Even if you'd give us back our guns, we'd still be

89

outnumbered three to one."

Canavan knew the odds were even worse than that. Molocek, Pixler, and Healey would have to be watched every minute unless they were left on the perimeter of the Apache camp without horses on which to make good their escape. Afoot they'd have to fight—or die.

He said, "I'm not out of my mind, and we are going to attack that camp. You three are going to help because you haven't got a choice. We'll take the horses with us and leave you on the north side of the Indian camp afoot. You'll fight or you'll be killed."

MacCorkindale asked, "And what about Edith Thorne?"

"If we don't attempt to rescue her, she's going to be taken into Mexico."

"But what if they kill her when we attack? You said—"

"I know it. I said they'd probably kill her if they got the chance. And they will. But she's sure as hell not going to survive a couple of years' captivity in Mexico. You know how these Apaches are treating her. You saw what she looked like the other night."

MacCorkindale nodded reluctantly. Canavan said, "I'm going on ahead and scout their camp. Wait here until I get back. It probably won't be much more than an hour. Be ready to move out. And keep an eye on Healey and those two bounty hunters."

MacCorkindale nodded. Canavan mounted and headed south in the direction the Apache band had gone.

A strange feeling of futility assailed him as he rode. Night before last he had done just what he was doing now. He had approached the Apache camp, hoping to rescue Edith Thorne. But tonight was different. Tonight he would commit everything to the rescue attempt.

Tomorrow morning they would either have Edith and be headed north, or they would all be dead. There could be nothing in between.

Two miles from where he had left the others, he reined in his horse. A feeling of uneasiness troubled him. He stared into the darkness ahead, puzzling at the cause of it.

He waited several minutes, while his eyes and ears strained. He heard nothing, saw nothing. But the uneasiness held.

With a little shrug, he touched the horse's sides with his heels and the animal moved ahead. Suddenly the horse turned his head slightly to one side. His ears pricked forward and his head came up . . .

Instantly, Canavan dug heels into him and reined him sharply to one side. A rifle flashed ahead and on his right. As if it were a signal, three other rifles flared.

Canavan's horse bolted, suddenly startled by the shots. Canavan crouched low over the horse's withers. His rifle was in his hand, but he made no attempt to fire it, knowing its muzzle flash would only give the Apaches their target.

He did not head straight back toward the place where the others were. Instead, he took a course at right angles, heading west. He figured he could shake off the Indians in the dark. He didn't want to lead them back to the others and let them find out how small was the force pursuing them.

His plan to attack the Apache camp had been hopeless, he supposed, from the start. It was probably a good thing he had been ambushed while heading for the Apache camp to scout.

His horse was tired from traveling all last night, and the Apaches were beginning to gain on them. For the first time Canavan felt a touch of concern. It was possible, he admitted, that he wouldn't get away. It was possible they'd catch up with him. But he continued for another mile as the distance between him and his pursuers diminished steadily.

There was only one thing left to do. Continuing along this course was hopeless. Whether he wanted to or not, he was going to have to lead the Indians back to where the others were. He could alert the others as he approached by firing his gun at the Indians, and by drawing their fire in return. He would have to take the chance that one of the Apaches might escape and tell the others that only six men were following.

Accordingly, he began gradually to turn, and shortly thereafter headed straight toward the place where MacCorkindale and the others were. Only a hundred yards now separated the four Indians from him.

His horse faltered, stumbled, recovered, and went on. A cold sweat drenched Canavan.

The camp lay ahead, no more than half a mile away. When he was only a quarter mile from it, with the Apaches fifty yards behind, Canavan suddenly turned in his saddle and began firing. He hit no one, nor had he expected to. Firing toward the rear from the back of a running horse in darkness made accuracy impossible. But his fire drew that of the Indians. They opened up on him recklessly. Canavan thundered past MacCorkindale and Hurley, swinging from his horse and whirling to face the oncoming Indians as he did.

The bounty hunters and Healey were vague and indistinct shapes in the darkness. He realized with a shock that there had been no time for MacCorkindale to give them back their guns. He yelled, "Down! Get down on the ground!"

The first of the pursuing Apaches thundered past less than half a dozen yards away. Canavan raised his rifle, following the galloping Indian with the muzzle, then pulling slightly ahead. He fired, leading the Indian by two feet the way he had sometimes led flying ducks with a shotgun back home in the east.

The Apache left the saddle, hit the ground with an audible thump and rolled in a flying cloud of dust. Canavan was running toward him even as a second Apache, lying low on his horse's withers, galloped through the camp, leaning far to one side to take a swipe at Canavan with his rifle butt. Canavan felt a rush of air passing less than an inch from his head. He grabbed the Indian's leg almost without thinking, but he could not hold on. Thrown off balance, he stumbled and rolled just as the Indian's gun fired at him from above. He came up as swiftly as possible to see that the Apache had skidded his horse to a halt and whirled. The horse was motionless for an instant, rearing—

Canavan snapped his rifle up and squeezed off a shot. The Indian lost his seat on the rearing horse and slid off his rump. The horse whirled and galloped away.

Canavan made it to his feet and rushed the Indian, hearing other shots and sounds of scuffling behind. The Indian he had shot off the rearing horse was still alive, rising. He swung his rifle and hit the Indian squarely on the ear with its stock. He could hear the skull caving in. The Indian collapsed.

Canavan ran toward the first Indian he had shot. Dead. Canavan turned.

MacCorkindale was walking toward him. He asked breathlessly, "How many were there, Mr. Canavan?"

"Four."

"Then we got them all. Hurley and I got two. Looks

like you got the other two."

A shadow came up from the ground and rushed toward one of the dead Indians. It was Healey and he snatched something from the ground and faded into the darkness beyond camp. His voice came floating back, harshly and triumphantly, "Don't any of you bastards try to follow me. I've got a gun and I'll sure as hell kill anybody that does!"

Molocek and Pixler got up from the ground where they had thrown themselves. "Lieutenant, give us our guns! Now! That son of a bitch is going to get away."

MacCorkindale said disgustedly, "Let him go. By God we've got more important things to do than chase after him!"

Canavan turned his back on the argument. He was looking for Neisha and there was sudden terror in his heart. Was it possible that she had accidentally been killed? He opened his mouth to call out her name.

THIRTEEN

HALF A DOZEN TIMES, CANAVAN CALLED NEISHA'S name. He got no reply. He heard Healey thunder away, the sounds of his horse's hoofs fading gradually into the night. Molocek and Pixler were arguing bitterly with MacCorkindale. "God damn you, Lieutenant, you got no right to keep us here against our will. We're civilians. You got no authority. We've put a couple of weeks of damn hard work into catching Healey. Now you're letting him get away!"

Caravan yelled, "Shut up, all of youl Have any of you seen Neisha since I've been gone?"

None of the four men had. Caravan made a swift

search of the camp area. The four Apaches still lay where they had fallen, but Caravan found no trace of the Indian girl.

He hurried to the picket line. Neisha's horse was gone.

Scowling furiously, he returned to camp. MacCorkindale said, "For Christ's sake, now what are we going to do?"

Caravan stared at him. The lieutenant's face was only a blur in the faint light from the stars. Caravan said, "I don't know what you're going to do, but I know what I'm going to do. I'm going to find Neisha. I just hope to God I find her before Healey does."

"You think Healey is after her?"

"I don't know. It's possible. Maybe he saw her leave. He hasn't got much chance of finding her in the dark, but when daylight comes—"

"What about Edith Thorne?"

Caravan said "Lieutenant, I took a long time making up my mind. Too long, or Neisha wouldn't have run away. But it's made up now. I don't intend to marry Edith Thorne."

"That doesn't relieve you of responsibility for what has happened to her."

"Maybe not. But I've got a responsibility to Neisha too."

"She's Apache. She can make her way back to your ranch by herself."

"Unless Healey gets her first."

"Healey's worrying more about his skin than he is about that Indian girl."

"The hell he is. Healey's been in Yuma for a long, long time. Neisha is the first woman he's seen since his escape."

95

"You can't find him in the dark any more than he can find the Indian girl."

"Maybe not, but I can try."

Molocek pleaded, "Lieutenant, let us go with him. You ain't got no chance of getting that white woman back anyway. Not now. Tomorrow them Apaches will be in Mexico."

MacCorkindale shook his head. "We're going on. We'll go into Mexico after them if it's necessary."

Caravan walked to his horse. He picked up the reins but he didn't mount. Maybe he could trail Healey in the dark. Maybe he could at least find out if Healey was trailing Neisha.

This time—if Healey molested Neisha *this* time, he promised himself that he would kill the man. He should have killed him last time. If he had, Neisha would not be in danger from him now.

He headed out of camp. Behind him, Lieutenant MacCorkindale said harshly, "Mr. Canavan!"

He ignored the lieutenant, who ordered, "Sergeant, go after him!"

Caravan called back, "Lieutenant, don't be a fool. I haven't got anything against Hurley, but by God if he tries to stop me I'll do whatever I have to do."

There was a moment's silence. Then Caravan heard the lieutenant say, "Never mind, Hurley. Let him go."

Even in the faint light from the stars, Caravan could see the deep indentations made by the hoofs of Healey's horse. He followed for half a mile, then stopped. He knelt and struck a match, cupping it with his hands. He studied the trail until the match burned his fingers. He dropped it and lighted another one.

He was following the trail of a single horse. He released a long, slow sigh of relief.

96

He veered right, leaving Healey's trail, looking for Neisha's trail instead. He traveled for half a mile without finding it. He knew he might have missed it in the dark, but he didn't think he had.

He retraced his steps to where he had left Healey's trail, and then veered left. He had gone no more than a quarter mile before he found the tracks of Neisha's horse.

Healey hadn't found her trail yet but he was heading north, just as Neisha was. When daylight came, he would probably be able to see her. He would almost certainly find her trail if he took time to look for it.

Canavan mounted and kicked his weary horse into a trot. He discovered that he could, without too much difficulty, stay with Healey's trail. Healey was forcing his horse to lope and as long as he maintained that gait his horse's tracks would be plain enough to follow even in the dark.

Canavan frowned with worry and concern. He knew how vicious Healey was. If the man got his hands on Neisha again it wouldn't do her any good to fight. Not unless she fought with a knife and even then Healey would probably have no trouble overpowering her.

For the first time, Canavan put himself in Neisha's place and realized how hard the last few days had been on her. She had believed that he intended to marry Edith Thorne as soon as they managed to rescue her. She had felt unwanted and alone.

If he'd only had the sense to tell her when he had made his decision. If only he had not delayed.

But he had delayed and now it was too late. Canavan was not a churchgoing man but suddenly he began to pray silently—that he would find Neisha before Healey did.

For the first half of the night, MacCorkindale stood guard over the disarmed bounty hunters, knowing they would slip away the first chance they got—even without guns. He believed, furthermore, that they would kill both him and Sergeant Hurley if it took that to get away. They might be operating within the law, but in MacCorkindale's judgment they were little better than Healey was. They slept, occasionally waking and looking at him to see if he had gone to sleep. He awakened Hurley at midnight, cautioning, "Stay awake, Sergeant. Those two will kill us both if they get the chance."

"Yes, Sir. You don't need to worry, Sir. I know they will."

MacCorkindale closed his eyes. He was near exhaustion and his shoulder ached continuously.

He wished desperately that he could release the bounty hunters and go back, but he knew that he could not. Even if continuing meant death for him, for Hurley and the two bounty hunters, he had to go on.

Was it only his career that concerned him? He tried to be completely honest with himself, and after some self-examination decided that other considerations had become more important to him than his career.

He discovered that being told by Canavan that he did not intend to marry Edith Thorne had caused considerable relief in him. He also discovered that he had no trouble conjuring up a picture of Edith Thorne's face in his mind. He smiled faintly to himself. Was it possible that he was falling in love, he who had been a bachelor all the thirty-three years of his life?

He pushed the thought away. Hell, he hadn't been with her but a few short hours the day the Apaches had captured her. He'd never talked to her at any length. It was physical attraction and nothing more. Yet he could not dismiss her from his thoughts. He could not get her face out of his mind.

He slept, an uneasy, tossing sleep that terminated as the eastern sky began to gray. Both he and Hurley were red-eyed and slack-jawed from weariness. The bounty hunters looked almost equally bad, but it was obvious that they had slept.

MacCorkindale sipped the scalding coffee Hurley had prepared. He hoped they would find water today. The canteens were nearly empty and the horses were suffering.

By the time the sun came up, they were in the saddle, riding south. MacCorkindale rode in the lead, followed by the bounty hunters. Hurley brought up the rear. Once Molocek called sourly, "Lieutenant, I'm going to see that charges are brought against you for holding us against our will."

MacCorkindale didn't bother to reply. He was concentrating on the trail, which the wind had obliterated in spots.

In midmorning, on the southern side of a tall, rocky cliff, they came upon a water seep, where a few trees grew, where there was green grass, where the Apaches had not been able to muddy the water because of the way it seeped out of the moss-grown rock. MacCorkindale called a halt.

They first let the horses drink. Then, patiently, they filled all the canteens from the trickle coming out of the rock. Then, when the pool had filled again, they let the horses drink a second time. The whole business consumed almost two hours because of the slowness with which the water seeped out of the rock.

But the rest was good for them. And while the men were filling their canteens, the horses greedily cropped every blade of green grass in sight.

Riding out, MacCorkindale wondered where the Mexican border was. For all he knew, they had already crossed it, and he was aware of the chance he took. If he was discovered by Mexican troops or *rurales*, he would be arrested and thrown in jail. He was wearing the uniform of the United States Army. Even if he was later released, he would face disciplinary action upon his return to the United States unless he managed to succeed. Unless he rescued Edith Thorne.

The odds against that were astronomical. They were only four, two of them unarmed. He wasn't even sure he dared arm the bounty hunters in the event they were attacked. He believed the bounty hunters capable of turning on Sergeant Hurley and himself.

Once more he thought of Edith Thorne. Her face haunted him. He remembered the way she had looked when he saw her last in the Apache camp. He remembered the Indian striking her . . .

Maybe they couldn't rescue her, he thought. Maybe the odds against them were too great to be overcome. But they were sure as hell going to try. He and Hurley and the bounty hunters were going to bring her back or they would not return themselves. Four men had already died defending Edith Thorne. If she remained to die in Mexico, those four lives had been thrown away.

And Canavan—he doubted if he'd see Canavan again. Or Healey. Or Canavan's Indian wife.

Nor was there now much chance of encountering the force that had ridden out of Fort Chiricahua several days ago. That force would stop at the Mexican border. They might send Apache scouts into Mexico, but the troops would not cross into Mexico themselves.

His face grim, his eyes narrowed against his continuous shoulder pain, Lieutenant MacCorkindale rode on, dusty, bearded, sweat-stained and rawhide-thin. Behind him, at ten-yard intervals, came the other three.

FOURTEEN

CANAVAN FOUND THAT HEALEY HAD TRAVELED NO more than a couple of miles at a lope. Then he had slowed to a trot, apparently satisfied that the bounty hunters were not pursuing him. His trail was more difficult to follow now since the horse's tracks were not as deeply impressed at a trot as they had been at a lope. Canavan was forced to slow his own horse to a walk, and to dismount sometimes and follow the trail afoot. He fumed at the delay because he knew every minute lost meant Healey was drawing farther away from him. Yet he did not dare leave the trail.

The night dragged on. At dawn, Canavan guessed he must be at least ten miles behind. He mounted, kicked his horse into a lope and raced northward along Healey's trail, in daylight plain and easily followed on horseback.

The sun was just poking its rim above the eastern mountains when Canavan suddenly yanked his horse to a halt. Healey's trail had merged with another coming from the left. For an instant Canavan held his breath. The second trail had been made by Neisha's horse. Having merged, the two trails stayed together, heading north.

Canavan's mouth was a grim line as he kicked his horse into a steady lope again. There was an emptiness in his belly and a coldness in his chest. Neisha might already be dead. She would have fought Healey for as long as she could. But Healey was strong and brutal and he would kill her if she fought too hard.

Canavan had forgotten how tired his horse was. The animal lagged, and stumbled, and Canavan had to slow him down. He dismounted, loosened the cinch and led the horse a while.

He cursed his helplessness. He prayed for Neisha as he had never before prayed for anything. He promised himself that if Healey had hurt her he'd kill him— slowly the way the Apaches would. He'd put a soaked strip of rawhide around Healey's head and stake him down in the sun and wait for the rawhide to dry, shrinking as it did. When Healey screamed and begged he'd laugh and remind the man of Neisha and what he had done to her.

He mounted again. It took all the will power he possessed to keep from kicking his horse into a lope again. The miles fell behind, five, ten . . .

And then he saw her. He swung from his horse and ran to where she was lying on her back in the pitiless desert sun.

Her face was a mass of welts and bruises put there by Healey's fists. Her clothes were all but torn off of her. But her chest rose and fell . . .

Canavan led his horse up beside her so that the horse's body shaded her from the sun. He got his canteen and soaked a piece of cloth he had torn from her skirt. He dabbed gently at her bruised and lacerated face. His throat constricted with pity and with love for her. But another emotion was stirring in him. It was a savage, burning hatred for the man who had done this to her.

Gently he held her. He put the canteen to her bruised and bleeding mouth, and let a little water trickle through. She choked, and coughed, and suddenly opened her eyes. They were filled with terror and her mouth opened to cry out. Then she saw who it was. The terror left her eyes and they filled suddenly with tears. She turned her face away from him. Her lips moved painfully but he was forced to lower his head so that he could hear what she was saying.

Her first words were indistinguishable. He held her closer, trying to understand; and at last he did. She was saying, "He should have killed me. I am ashamed. I am so ashamed!"

His arms drew her even closer to him. He lowered his head and laid his unshaven cheek against her own. He said sternly, "You will never say that again! It is my fault this has happened to you. It is my fault you ran away. I have been a fool because I didn't take the time to confide in you."

Her body still shook with sobs. He said, "I do not want the white woman. I asked her to marry me long ago before I knew you. She will go back to the East when we get her away from the Apaches and I will go back to Furnace Creek with you. We have been married according to Apache law. Now we will be married according to the white man's law."

"I cannot come back to you. Not after what that man has done to me."

"You will heal and you will forget. It means nothing because it was done against your will. It means nothing."

Slowly, slowly, her shaking quieted. "What will we do now?"

"Go on and follow Healey's tracks."

"You will kill him? Is that not against the white man's law?"

"The law won't care. There's a bounty on his head, dead or alive."

"She struggled to her feet and began trying to repair her clothes. He couldn't help her and it was makeshift business at best because she had neither needle nor thread. But she managed to mend them so that they covered her. Canavan mounted, then lifted her up behind him. He headed west along Healey's trail. He knew it could not long continue toward the west because that was where Yuma lay. He would have to turn either north or south.

If north, Canavan would follow and the rescue of Edith would have to be carried out by Lieutenant MacCorkindale If south, it was possible he might make contact later with MacCorkindale. But wherever Healey's trail went, Canavan would follow it.

Ten miles west, the trail turned south. Canavan grunted to himself with satisfaction. He had figured south. There was safety in Mexico for Healey and with the border this close, he'd have been a fool to go anyplace else.

Neisha did not complain. She sat behind him silently, one arm around his waist. Several times he asked solicitously if she was all right and each time she said she was. But he knew the sun hurt her battered face cruelly. He knew every movement the horse made hurt her bruised and battered body.

He fixed his eyes grimly on the horizon ahead.

Leading Neisha's horse, Healey rode straight west for what he judged to be a dozen miles. He intended, eventually, to cut south toward Mexico. He had only

104

headed north last night because that was the way the squaw had gone. He had been in prison for a long time and last night catching her had seemed even more important to him than escape. Besides, he had doubted if anyone would pursue him. He doubted if MacCorkindale was going to let the bounty hunters go.

Leading the horse Neisha had been riding and in possession of her knife and a rifle, he felt better this morning than he had for a long, long time. The squaw had put up quite a fight, but that had only added zest to the experience. He supposed he ought to have brought her along with him, but he hadn't wanted to take the chance that she might slow him down. Besides, he hadn't felt able to trust her. She'd have tried to kill him every time he closed his eyes.

He knew that the squaw might die back there where he had left her. She had neither water nor a horse. She was badly beaten and traveling would be difficult. Unless she was found by some of her own people, she would die.

He didn't push his horse. There wasn't any hurry now. But he did occasionally look behind, searching the horizon for a telltale lift of dust.

He saw nothing. He covered forty miles by nightfall and made camp in a little canyon that held a scattering of trees and a seep that, when dug out, filled with enough water to let the horses drink and to let Healey fill both his own canteen and the one he had taken from the squaw.

He found jerky in the squaw's saddlebags, and coffee, and a piece of salt pork. He broke some dry branches off the trees and built a fire. He heated water and made coffee, and then fried some of the salt pork. He put dry biscuits in the grease and fried them crisp.

He had finished eating and was drinking the last of the coffee when the first Apache rode into his camp. Healey dived for his rifle, but stopped when he saw the others. He was soon surrounded by more than a dozen Apache braves sitting on their horses within a dozen yards of him.

He raised his hands and tried to grin at them. Hell, he'd have thought these damned renegades would have been fifty miles south of here by now.

Two of them dismounted, walked to him, and picked his rifle up. Too late Healey remembered that he had taken it from one of the Indians that had chased Canavan into camp yesterday. The Indians examined the rifle, talking together in the Apache tongue. Healey couldn't understand what they said but he understood well enough what was going on. They recognized the rifle as belonging to one of their friends. They had guessed the Indian who owned the gun was dead and that this white man was responsible for his death.

Healey suddenly wished he had made a fight of it. They'd have killed him if he had, he knew, but right now he had an uneasy feeling they were going to kill him anyway. And his dying might take all night.

One of the dismounted Apaches drew his knife. Holding it at waist level, he approached Healey. Healey backed up, a slow step at a time. More than ever he wished he had not given up so easily. Only God knew what they were going to do to him.

He backed, wanting to whirl and run, but resisting the desire. Until at last he could resist no more. He turned and ran, trying to dodge between two Apache horses, failing because their riders reined them together and blocked his way.

He tried to turn and fight but it was too late. The

Indians were on him, and in seconds his hands were tied behind his back. He struggled but it was no use. He could smell them and he wished the one who had the knife would use it, but the man did not except to make grinning passes with it at Healey's groin.

Now all the Apaches dismounted. Some brought rawhide thongs. Others brought stakes that they drove into the ground with rocks. His hands were freed and the thongs tied to his wrists and ankles. He was spread-eagled on the ground, tied to the stakes, stretched out as broadly as the Apaches could stretch him out.

They built fires now, seeming to forget him for a time. They dug out the seep and watered their horses and filled their own skin water bags. Over the fires they cooked some horsemeat they had with them and ate it, grinning at each other and chattering back and forth in the Apache tongue. Sometimes one of them would point to Healey and grin, or make an obscene gesture to indicate what they meant to do to him.

Healey's body felt cold as ice despite the heat in the ground under him, despite the still, hot air.

Finished with their eating, the Indians clustered around him. They squatted on the ground. They took out their knives and began whetting them. They grinned at each other and they made more gestures to indicate what Healey could expect.

He began to beg them to set him free. He told them to look at his ankles. He had been a prisoner of the white men just as they had, he said. He hated the white men as much as they did. Some of them got up and looked at the manacle scars on his ankles. One scooped up a coal from the fire. Grinning, he carried it to Healey and carefully dropped it on Healey's belly.

It took only a split second to burn through Healey's

shirt. He opened his mouth and released a long, sustained scream. He screamed, and screamed, and he smelled the burning of his own flesh combining with the smell of burning cloth. Even after the coal had cooled, he continued to scream until one of the Apaches kicked him in the head.

He was half unconscious. He seemed to hear them talking from far away. His belly was a continuous area of pain.

Time passed. At last he felt one of them raise his head. He wondered what they were going to do now. Whatever it was, it didn't hurt. It felt as though they were putting a bandage around his head. But why were they doing that? They hadn't hurt his head. Why were they putting a bandage around it then?

They dropped his head. One of them threw water into his face. The shock of it brought him back to full consciousness. The bandage around his head felt tight.

They stood around him in a circle, grinning savagely down at him. And then, suddenly, he heard words spoken to him in English. For an instant, hope flared in him, but it died as he recognized the laborious way the words were spoken, as he realized what the speaker was telling him.

"We go now. You feel fine till sun come up. Then rawhide shrink and dry. Hurt head. You mebbe die. Pretty slow."

Fear didn't touch Healey yet. He figured once they had gone, he could free his hands. He lay still, listening, and heaved a long, slow sigh of relief when they rode away.

He began struggling with his bonds. If he could free only one hand, if he could pull only one of the stakes they had driven into the ground . . .

But, stretched out this way, he could get no leverage. And the more he pulled against the rawhide thongs, the tighter they became. His hands and feet grew numb as his own struggling cut off the blood from them. And at last the sun came up.

It was bearable for a while. The drying of the rawhide band around his head was slow. It was only a small headache at first, growing in intensity until—

He screamed, the way he had when they dropped the coal upon his belly last night. He screamed until he ran out of breath and could scream no more. Even then his mouth remained open and he went on screaming silently . . .

FIFTEEN

CANAVAN FOUND HEALEY SPREAD-EAGLED, FACE UP in the burning afternoon sun. At first he thought the man was dead. He saw the hole burned in Healey's shirt front and the burn beneath. He saw the cruel strip of rawhide around Healey's head. Drying, it had almost buried itself in the flesh.

The man's eyes were open, but he was blind from the burning rays of the sun. Then Canavan saw movement in his chest.

Maybe he wasn't going to be cheated after all. Healey might not be able to see him, but if he could be revived enough to know who Canavan was, if he knew he was going to be killed and why, then there might still be some a satisfaction in it.

He dismounted and walked to Healey, drawing his knife as he did. He knelt, and as carefully as possible, cut the rawhide thong around Healey's head. He had to pull it loose, so deeply was it buried in the flesh. He went on to cut Healey's hands and feet loose, noting that they were gray from lack of blood. Healey was going to have gargrene in both hands and both feet even if he lived. He'd never walk or use his hands. He'd never see again.

Canavan said, "Healey. Know who this is?"

Healey did not move. The only sign of life was the faint rise and fall of his chest. Canavan turned his head and looked at Neisha.

She wasn't looking at him. She was staring down at Healey instead. Caravan had expected hatred in her eyes, revulsion at the very least, but neither emotion was visible. Nor was pity. She looked at Healey without feeling, without emotion of any kind. It was as though Healey was already dead.

He had his canteen and poured water into Healey's face. It had no visible effect. And then Healey's chest stopped rising and falling. Canavan knelt and picked up his wrist. He could find no pulse. Healey was dead.

He had wanted to kill Healey, to punish him for what he had done to Neisha. Now he realized that the Apaches had done it for him, done it in a way he never could. Last night Healey had paid for all his sins. He had paid more than either Canavan or the law would have required him to pay.

Canavan dug out the seep. He waited a few minutes for the water to clear, then filled all the canteens, his and the two Healey had been carrying. Both Healey's horse and Neisha's were gone, taken by the Indians.

Next, he watered his horse. After that, while the horse grazed, he scooped out a shallow grave in the soft sand, with sticks and flat rocks, and rolled Healey's body into it. He covered the grave, stood up and looked at Neisha. "Do you want to go home now?"

110

She shook her head.

"Where do you want to go?"

"We should try to find the lieutenant. We should help him get the white woman back."

He nodded. He mounted, then lifted her up behind him. He headed south again. Sooner or later these Apaches would rendezvous with the ones who had captured Edith Thorne. When they did, he would find Lieutenant MacCorkindale, Sergeant Hurley and the two bounty hunters. If the Apaches hadn't found them first.

He stopped at dark and cooked a meager meal for Neisha and himself. He made coffee and killed the fire, and after a couple of hours' rest led out again. He traveled at a slow walk throughout most of the night, dismounting and walking often to spare the horse.

The trail began climbing now, into rocky, mostly barren mountains, but as the altitude steadily increased, so did the grass available for grazing. At dawn, Canavan stopped in a little grassy draw and dug out a damp place so that water seeped up and filled the hole. He gave the horse two hours to graze and drink. With the animal picketed, he lay down with Neisha to sleep.

The heat of the sun beating directly down on him woke him up. He got up, roused Neisha, and they went on.

He supposed they were now in Mexico, although he had no way of being sure. But he kept a careful vigil, scouting the horizon before he would cross a ridge, traveling whenever possible in low places where they could not be seen.

This day passed, and the next, and on the third day he found where the renegades they were following had rendezvoused with another band. And this evening, before it grew too dark, he left Neisha and scouted for the trail left by MacCorkindale, Hurley, and the bounty hunters.

He did not find their trail, but he knew if the others were still following the Indians, they would be along. He therefore returned to Neisha. They slept, and in the morning waited in camp, Neisha repairing her clothes while he kept watch.

At ten, he saw MacCorkindale, Hurley, and the two bounty hunters riding toward him out of the north. They looked exhausted. Their horses plodded along listlessly, heads down. They were leading three extra horses. MacCorkindale's face brightened when he saw Canavan. He looked beyond, at Neisha, taking in the bruises and scabbed lacerations on her face. Nor did the bounty hunters miss the way she looked. Their eyes immediately began to search the area behind Canavan for their prisoner.

MacCorkindale said, "I'm sorry, Canavan. Where is he now?"

Molocek broke in, "Yeah. Where is he? You didn't turn him loose for Christ's sake?"

Canavan shook his head. "I didn't turn him loose."

"Didn't you catch him? Did he get away?"

Again Canavan shook his head. "No. I found him all right. Only the Indians had found him first."

"Is he dead?"

"He's dead."

Molocek said incredulously, "And you buried him? Do you know how much he's worth?"

Canavan said, "You said a hundred dollars, didn't you?"

"A hundred dollars hell! He's worth a thousand bucks!"

"He's dead. And I buried him."

"Where? For God's sake, where? We can still dig him up and take him back."

MacCorkindale interrupted him. "You're going along with us. You're going to stick with us until we get that woman away from the Indians."

Molocek stared at MacCorkindale unbelievingly. "You can go straight to hell! You can't keep us now! If we don't get to Healey right away, he'll rot and we'll never be able to prove who he is!"

MacCorkindale stared at Molocek with disgust. Pixler said something under his breath to Molocek. Molocek said, "You're going to have to shoot to stop us, Lieutenant. We're going to backtrack Canavan until we find the place he buried Healey. Come on, Pixler. Let's get going." He turned his horse and started away.

MacCorkindale looked at Canavan helplessly. Canavan said, "Let them go, Lieutenant. They're not likely to be any good to us anyway."

MacCorkindale nodded reluctantly. He called, "Molocek!"

The bounty hunter turned.

MacCorkindale said, "Sergeant, give their guns back to them. I wouldn't send even a bounty hunter out onto that desert unarmed."

Hurley returned the bounty hunters' guns. The two rode away toward the north, questing back and forth like hounds until they had picked up the trail made by Caravan earlier.

MacCorkindale looked at Canavan. "It's pretty stupid to go on. There are only three of us and there are at least thirty Indians."

Canavan shrugged.

"What do you want to do?"

113

Canavan shrugged again. "You're in charge."

"If we're south of the border, we'll get no help. Colonel Meagher wouldn't cross the border. Not without express authority."

Caravan nodded agreement.

"And if we're caught by the Mexican *rurales* or by Mexican soldiers, we'll probably get thrown in jail."

Canavan said, "On the other hand, Edith has no hostage value any more. If she doesn't work hard enough to suit them, they'll kill her."

MacCorkindale said, "Maybe it's better that she should die than that all of us should."

Canavan waited. He knew it was foolish to keep on. He could see no possible way of rescuing Edith Thorne.

MacCorkindale said, "I guess it's up to each of you. How many want to go back?"

No one answered him. He asked, "How many want to go on?"

Hurley nodded unenthusiastically. "I guess if the rest of you are stupid enough to, then I am too." Caravan grunted assent. Neisha nodded her head when the lieutenant looked at her. MacCorkindale said, "We'll probably all get killed."

Caravan said, "Your four troopers got killed. The Flores family got killed. Every time I think about going back, I think about the Flores family." He knew his words made little sense. The three of them and Neisha were certainly not going to put a stop to the depredations of the Apache renegades. They weren't even going to rescue Edith Thorne. Not unless, by some miracle, they got help.

MacCorkindale nodded. "All right then, let's go."

Neisha mounted one of the Indian ponies. Hurley led the other two. Caravan took the lead and they headed south once more.

SIXTEEN

NEISHA WAS OBVIOUSLY SUFFERING FROM HER injuries. The horses were gaunt and near exhaustion. The men were worn and gaunt themselves, even though their wounds seemed to be healing satisfactorily. Their food, which had been used sparingly for days, was now almost gone. Canavan knew something would have to be done, and soon, to replenish their supplies.

Believing themselves safe in Mexico, the Apaches were now traveling at a more leisurely pace. And since Canavan was in no hurry to catch up, he halted often, trying to stay a day behind. Sooner or later, he supposed, the Apaches would reach whatever sanctuary they were heading for. When that time came, he and MacCorkindale would have to decide what they were going to do.

Perhaps they should risk contacting the Mexican authorities. The Mexicans had no love for Apaches. They feared and hated them as much as did the Americans. The Mexican army might be persuaded to launch an attack on the renegades. And if they knew what the situation was they might even permit the troops from Fort Chiricahua to cross the border.

The country grew rockier and more rugged as they continued south. Down to only enough food for one more meal, Canavan told MacCorkindale, "Stay in camp today and let the horses graze. I'm going to see if I can get a deer."

He left shortly before sunup, smiling reassuringly at Neisha as he left. Her face still showed the marks of Healey's fists, but the swelling had gone down. She was busy at the fire, cooking breakfast for Hurley and

115

MacCorkindale.

He rode into the mountains, following first one canyon and then another. He kept his eyes mostly on the ground, looking for tracks, but he also scrutinized the horizon and the hillsides at regular intervals. He had gone nearly a dozen miles before he saw the first deer tracks among the scrub trees and brush on the canyon floor. Canavan slid his rifle out of the saddle scabbard and climbed his horse onto the hillside to his right so that he could see any deer that he might flush out.

He was concerned about firing his gun because he knew the sound of it would carry. But he hadn't seen any tracks other than those made by the deer and he knew the Apaches were far ahead.

Suddenly a buck deer bounded out of the brush at the bottom of the canyon on his left. Immediately he slid out of his saddle, knelt, and drew a careful bead. He held himself still, ready to fire but not firing, hoping the deer would stop. He couldn't afford to miss. They needed the meat desperately and this was the only deer that he had seen. Besides, he didn't want to fire any more shots than were necessary.

The deer bounded up the slope for fifty yards. Suddenly it stopped and turned its head to stare at Canavan and his horse. Canavan squeezed his shot off carefully. He heard the bullet hit and saw the deer go to his knees. The animal collapsed on its side, kicked a couple of times, and then lay still. The report of Canavan's rifle echoed and reechoed from the rocky canyon walls.

He remained still for a time, watchfully scanning the ridge in front of him and the one behind. He saw nothing move. He heard nothing. Satisfied that his shot had not been heard either by Mexicans or Indians, he mounted and rode to where the buck deer lay.

Again he scanned the ridge tops on both sides of him. Then he knelt and quickly dressed the deer. He led his horse to the downhill side of the carcass, lifted it and laid it across the horse's back. He cut a hole between two of the deer's ribs and pushed the saddle horn up through the hole. Mounting behind the deer, he headed back in the direction he had come.

He kept thinking uneasily about the way his rifle shot had echoed. The sound could have carried as much as a mile but even though he doubted if anyone could have been within a mile of him to hear, his uneasiness did not abate. Every now and then he looked behind, searching the rocky mountaintops.

Once, he thought he saw something move. He watched the spot for several minutes without seeing anything. Shrugging, he kicked his horse into a trot and headed back toward camp where he arrived in midafternoon. The faces of all three who had remained in camp lighted when they saw the deer. Canavan halted and slid off. Neisha came forward immediately. She knelt beside the carcass, knife in hand.

Canavan unsaddled his horse and picketed him to graze. He caught himself still watching the rocky slopes. MacCorkindale asked, "Is something wrong?"

Canavan shook his head. "I don't think so. I didn't see anything and I didn't hear anything but—Hell, I guess I'm getting nervous from following Apaches too long."

Hurley had been gathering firewood. He brought an armload of it and built up the fire so that Neisha could cook some meat. A thin column of smoke rose into the air. Canavan opened his mouth to tell Hurley to cut down on the smoke. He closed it again without saying

117

anything. There was no use making everyone nervous just because he was. Chances were there wasn't a soul within fifty miles. He'd seen no tracks. He had no reason to believe otherwise.

The smell of cooking venison filled the air. Suddenly Canavan's horse, a hundred yards from camp, raised his head and nickered. His head was turned toward the north. His ears were pricked forward and alert.

Canavan dived for his rifle, which he had laid aside. He bawled, "MacCorkindale! Hurley! Neisha! Get behind those rocks!"

He sprinted toward the rocks, throwing himself to the ground behind them just as the first shot cracked, just as the first bullet kicked dust from the rock it had hit.

A fusillade now crackled, and other bullets struck and ricocheted away into space. Canavan cursed angrily. If he only hadn't killed the deer! His shot must have drawn these attackers here. But who were they? Indians or Mexicans?

As if in answer to his question, a voice called, "Señores! Throw down your guns! You are trespassing in Mexico and are under arrest!"

MacCorkindale, flat on his stomach a dozen yards away, turned and looked at Canavan. Canavan shook his head. "Mexican troops wouldn't have shot from ambush, lieutenant."

"That's what I was thinking. Who are they, then?"

"Bandits. They want our horses and guns."

"Any suggestions?"

"Try holding them off until dark. Then maybe we can get away."

The voice called, "Señores! Surrender or we must kill you all!"

Neither Canavan nor any of the others bothered to

reply. Into the Mexican's voice when he next yelled at them had come a savage edge, "Very well, Señores. If you must die then you must die."

For a time after that there was no sound. Canavan could hear the Mexicans conversing with each other in Spanish, but he could not make out what was said. He turned his head and looked behind. There was no cover for the Mexicans back there so they weren't going to be outflanked or surrounded, not at least until it grew dark.

Neisha lay next to him, crouched low behind a rock. She kept her head down but her face was turned toward him. She was watching him, not afraid, filled with confidence that he would in some way get them safely out of this.

He smiled ruefully at her, wishing he were as confident. And suddenly he faced the incredible foolhardiness of this whole expedition. They had no business being here. The Apaches outnumbered them ten to one. They could expect no help from the troopers out of Fort Chiricahua because those troops had already turned back. They could expect no help from the Mexicans. They would encounter no Mexican regulars, no *rurales*. Even if they defeated the bandits now besieging them, or got away, they still must cope with thirty Apache renegades.

Why, then, did he not simply tell MacCorkindale that he was going back? It would certainly be the simplest way out of this predicament. Then he thought of Edith Thorne. She had come west relying on his earlier promise to marry her. It was not her fault that the Apaches had captured her. Could he return with Neisha and live with her knowing Edith was a prisoner in Mexico, living an existence that for a white woman could not help but be intolerable? He shook his head reluctantly.

He felt MacCorkindale watching him and turned his head. The lieutenant grinned through his cracked lips. His face was sunburned and dusty, his eyes an incredible blue peering at Canavan. He said, "We've got to be the two stupidest men alive. Not that we're going to be alive for very long. I've been lying here wondering what the hell I'm doing here."

Canavan nodded. "So have I."

MacCorkindale said, "I haven't been fair to the rest of you. I lost four men when the Apaches jumped us and captured Miss Thorne and I've been willing to sacrifice all of you to vindicate myself. I figured if I could just get her back, then nobody would say it had been my fault. But it was my fault. Nothing I do now will change that fact. I may get Miss Thorne back and if I do I may get a medal pinned on me for it, but those four men I lost are going to haunt me until I die."

Canavan didn't say anything. Nothing he could say would change the situation as far as the lieutenant was concerned. He was in a similar fix himself. Even if he managed to rescue Edith and take her back, he would never be able to completely forgive himself for the ordeal she had endured because of him. And if she died or was killed before they could rescue her . . . His own guilt would be intolerable.

He could see the horses fidgeting ahead, between the bandits and themselves. They were out of the line of fire, but barely so. They would be the bandits' first objective as soon as the light faded. If they managed to capture the horses the bandits would probably withdraw, knowing the Americans would die on foot.

He glanced at MacCorkindale, then at the sun already nearing the horizon in the west. He said, "As soon as it

120

gets dark enough, they're going to make a try for our horses. If they get them, they may pull out and leave us here afoot."

MacCorkindale didn't reply. Canavan said, "Soon as I figure I can move without getting shot, I'm going out. Our only chance is to get the horses before they do and get the hell out of here. Maybe we can outrun them in the dark."

"I'll go with you."

"No. You stay here. There's no sense in both of us getting shot. If one can't do it, then two can't either."

Once more the voice of the English-speaking bandit came from ahead. "Señores! We do not want to kill anyone. Surrender and no harm will come to you."

The sun had dropped behind the mountains in the west. Shade marched across the desert floor. Canavan could see his saddle a dozen feet from the fire. He could see the canteen hanging from the saddle horn. He could smell the cooking venison. The fire had died to a smoldering bed of coals.

The color faded from the sky, and dusk deepened gradually. At last, when the horses were but shadowy outlines, Canavan raised himself carefully. He laid his rifle on the ground. He drew his revolver from its holster at his side. Then without speaking to the others, he stood up and crept forward toward the horses. He eased the hammer of his revolver back.

He traveled swiftly now, knowing the bandits would waste no time once they figured it was dark enough. He reached his horse and quickly untied the picket rope. A horse farther from him started suddenly. He whirled to face the sound when the muzzle of a gun jabbed cruelly into his back, forcing a gust of breath from him. A voice said, "Do not move, Señor, or you will die."

Canavan froze. The voice said, "Your gun, Señor."

He released the gun as the man's hand closed over it. He heard the hammer ease softly down.

The man said, "Now call to your friends to surrender or I will put a big hole in your belly where it will hurt the most."

Canavan said, "Don't talk about it, put it there. I'm not going to tell anybody to surrender."

The rifle jabbed into his back hard enough to make him gasp with pain. The voice said, "Tell them! You have only a few more seconds to live if you do not!"

SEVENTEEN

CANAVAN CLENCHED HIS JAWS. HE SAID NOTHING AND waited for the bullet to smash into him. He'd had a couple of encounters with Mexican bandits before and he knew they were capable of that kind of cold-blooded murder. He said, "You've got the horses and you've got my gun. Take them and let us go."

"Ah, Señor, you would like that, would you not? But we are not blind. We know you have a woman along with you. You have saddles and more guns and you have meat cooking over your fire."

Canavan yelled, "MacCorkindale!"

The bandit struck him on the side of the head with the muzzle of his gun. "Silence! You will speak when I tell you to speak."

The bandit called out, "Señor MacCorkindale! Your *companero* is my prisoner. Unless you surrender immediately he will die."

Canavan heard MacCorkindale's voice, "And what if we surrender?"

"Ah, Señor, we only wish to live. Your horses and guns and food are all we want from you. If you surrender, you will all be safe."

Canavan opened his mouth to yell at MacCorkindale to refuse. The bandit's gun barrel struck him a second time on the side of the head, this time with enough force to make his head reel, to put a brassy taste into his mouth. The words died on his lips. He heard MacCorkindale yell, "All right. You can have everything."

Canavan was dragged into camp. The five bandits immediately collected guns from MacCorkindale, Hurley, and Neisha. One of them piled wood on the fire. They were apparently in high spirits over their success. They laughed and helped themselves to the venison which was, by now, partly burned.

Canavan's head ached ferociously. He looked at MacCorkindale. "That was stupid, Lieutenant," he whispered. "They're not going to let us live. Besides the guns and horses, they want Neisha and they're not going to get her. At least not while I've alive."

MacCorkindale said, "It wasn't stupid. It was the only thing I could do. Without horses we're all finished anyway. I gave up to buy a little time. By God, if I hadn't, you'd be dead."

"What good is the time you bought? They've got our guns."

One of the bandits came to them, gun in hand, grinning at Canavan and then looking Neisha over insolently. He approached her and reached out for her, still grinning, still insolent. Suddenly Neisha jerked one knee at him with great force. The bandit let out a cry that was almost a scream and collapsed. He rolled on the ground, hugging his belly, groaning.

The English-speaking bandit rushed toward Neisha, his revolver in his hand. She waited, her expression anticipating a blow. Canavan grunted, "All right, Lieutenant. This is what you bought."

He made a running dive at the bandit, who came whirling around immediately. One of the others shouted something in Spanish from the fire and a rifle roared. Hurley and MacCorkindale stopped abruptly, turning their heads toward the bandit with the rifle. Slowly, MacCorkindale raised his hands.

But Canavan was in motion and couldn't have stopped if he had wanted to. He struck the bandit in the knees with his shoulder and brought him down in a heap. The revolver discharged into the air. He rolled, trying to get his feet under him, expecting a bullet to smash into him momentarily.

But Neisha had moved when he did and now she leaped upon the downed bandit, wrenching his gun out of his hands as she sank her teeth into his wrist. The bandit yelled with pain.

A swift glance at MacCorkindale and Hurley showed Canavan how helpless they had been to intervene. Three guns were aimed at them. If they tried to help, they would be riddled before they had gone two steps.

Neisha tried to get away, holding the bandit's revolver, but he caught her from behind. She flung the gun toward Canavan and he dived for it. His hand closed over it—At the fire, the rifle roared again. The bullet dug up a shower of dirt beside his outstretched hand. He froze, lying prone, his hand holding on to the gun. The rifle roared again, and this time the dirt it kicked covered Canavan's wrist and hand. He released the gun and drew back his hand.

There was no leering insolence in the bandit's face as

124

he released Neisha and struggled to his feet. There was only fury. He raised his arm and stared at the bleeding teeth marks on his wrist. He cursed and slapped Neisha savagely.

Covered by three guns from the fire, Canavan didn't move. The English-speaking bandit, who was apparently the leader, spoke to the others in Spanish. One of them went to his horse and took down his rawhide lariat. Grinning, he flung the loop over the arm of a giant saguaro at the edge of the circle of firelight.

Another came to where Canavan stood, got behind him, and shoved his rifle muzzle into Canavan's back. The bandit leader took a piece of rawhide from his saddlebags, and tied Canavan's wrists behind him. He pulled the rawhide as tight as he could, and Canavan gritted his teeth to keep from crying out.

It was plain that they meant to hang him from the arm of that saguaro, and if the others tried to intervene, they'd be shot down. Not that failing to intervene would save their lives. They'd be shot anyway before the bandits left. Only Neisha would remain alive. They'd take her with them; and if she fought they'd kill her too.

Canavan waited with a calmness he didn't feel. He could see no way of gaining the upper hand. He could see no hope. He'd faced death before but never had it seemed as certain as it did right now. He had always been able to fight—One of the bandits brought his horse, and indicated that he was to mount. Canavan growled, "How the hell do you expect me to get up on that horse? My hands are tied."

Two of them tried to boost him up. Canavan made himself go limp. The bandit leader said, "Señor, if you don't get on that horse, we have other ways of killing you. Ways worse than hanging, take my word."

125

Still Canavan did not help. The bandit said, "Your woman. Would you like to see her cut a little with my knife?"

Canavan shrugged. "All right. Boost me up." He raised a foot into the stirrup and let the bandits boost him into his saddle. A third one, on horseback, now rode close and, when Canavan's horse was led beneath the saguaro, put the noose over his head.

The bandit leader took the end of the rope in his hands and yanked, tightening it cruelly. Canavan sat very still, watching out of the corner of his eye as the bandit leader wound the rope around the base of the saguaro.

He glanced at Neisha. Her eyes, wide, stricken, told him that she would die when he died, in spirit if not in body. He looked at MacCorkindale. There was wildness in MacCorkindale's eyes and he realized that the lieutenant wasn't going to permit the hanging. Not as long as he was alive. He was going to try putting up a fight.

Canavan held his breath. At the first startling movement, or the moment a shot was fired, this horse was going to bolt right out from under him. It was fidgeting nervously as it was, alternately straining on the rope around Canavan's neck and slackening it.

He wanted to yell, to curse. He clenched his jaws and remained silent. Tensely he waited.

EIGHTEEN

THE BANDIT LEADER NOW SLOUCHED TOWARD THE horse, a quirt in his hand. He was grinning, but his eyes were cold.

126

The fire still blazed high, illuminating the scene with its flickering light. Neisha made no sound. Everyone seemed to be waiting helplessly for something they felt powerless to stop.

The bandit leader reached the horse and raised the quirt. It descended and Canavan heard it strike the horse's rump. The startled horse leaped ahead. The rope bit cruelly into his throat and he was jerked from the horse's back. He choked, and gagged, and he felt as though his neck was broken, but the fact that he was still conscious told him it was not. The bandits had not bothered to fashion a hangman's noose at the end of the rope. The fact that they hadn't had so far saved his life.

His lungs labored, trying to draw in air but his throat was closed by the rope's constricting pressure and no air got through. As he began to kick helplessly his body swung against the saguaro trunk and the spines penetrated his clothes and flesh. He scarcely felt them. His lungs were burning as if a fire had been kindled in his chest. Suddenly his ears filled with sound, a roaring that at first he thought resulted from his lack of air. But gradually they became separate sounds, the sounds of gunshots, and of shouts.

He felt someone touch his dangling legs, felt a pair of sturdy shoulders beneath him, lifting him, taking some of the deadly pressure off his neck. He gasped and labored, trying to draw air into his lungs. The noose slackened ever so slightly, but it was enough. Life-giving air flowed into his lungs and out again with a harshly rasping sound. He was alive. He had been hanged, but he was still, miraculously, alive!

The shots continued, and the shouts, but the language was Spanish which he did not understand except for an occasional word or two. From beneath him he heard

127

MacCorkindale say, "Steady, man, steady. Hang on a minute until your woman cuts the rope."

Suddenly he felt the rope go slack. He fell, bringing MacCorkindale down with him. MacCorkindale immediately seized him and dragged him behind the saguaro trunk, where Neisha and Hurley already were. The four crouched there together while Canavan gagged and choked helplessly. Tears filled his eyes and ran across his cheeks. He felt a knife sawing at the rawhide with which the bandit had tied his hands, and an instant later he was free. His hands were numb, but he knew that soon they would hurt badly enough. He reached up and laboriously removed the noose from around his neck.

MacCorkindale said, "Those are either Mexican Army troopers or *rurales*. They jumped the bandits just about the time that son of a bitch whipped the horse out from under you. I thought we were all finished, but it looks like maybe we aren't. Not yet at least."

The bandits had crouched behind the same rocks where Canavan and the others had taken cover earlier in the day. Bullets ricocheted from them and whined into space. One of the bandits, hit, stood up. He was riddled instantly by a dozen bullets. Literally driven back by their force, he sprawled, twitched a couple of times and then lay still, drenching the ground with blood.

Canavan's hands were throbbing painfully and the fingers were difficult to move. Sick at his stomach, he crawled weakly away from the others, gagging and vomiting. Neisha came with him and knelt beside him, her hands cool against his sweat-soaked forehead.

Another of the bandits, hit, cried out with shock and pain, then fell dead. Only three of them now were left, the leader and two others; these threw out their guns and raised their hands. As they slowly got to their feet calling out, MacCorkindale, who knew Spanish, translated that they wished to surrender, and that they had done no wrong except to capture these *Americano* intruders whom they had meant to turn over to the authorities.

Canavan, still violently sick, had crawled back near the saguaro trunk. He lay there gasping helplessly as the Mexican troopers came cautiously into camp. They searched the remaining bandits roughly for concealed weapons. Their commander, a lieutenant, detailed a guard to watch them, then approached the group at the foot of the saguaro.

MacCorkindale stood up. Hurley stood just behind him. Both saluted and MacCorkindale said in Spanish, "I am Lieutenant MacCorkindale of the United States Army. This is Sergeant Hurley. We are most grateful for your timely arrival, believe me, Sir."

Canavan could not force himself to his feet. He still felt weak and sick. His throat, from which the skin had been peeled by the rope, burned and ached. He swallowed frequently and each time he winced with pain.

The Mexican lieutenant was of medium height, and slender. He looked no more than twenty-five years old. Without a smile he asked harshly, "What are you doing in Mexico?"

"We have been following a band of Apache renegades who escaped from the reservation near Fort Chiricahua, Arizona Territory. They captured a white woman I was escorting and killed four of the troopers with me."

The Mexican lieutenant stared coldly at him, then shifted his glance to Hurley. Lastly he approached

Canavan and looked down at him. He turned his head and asked MacCorkindale, "Who is he? And why were they hanging him? Is he an outlaw, a murderer?"

"None of those things, Sir. He is our civilian guide. The Indian woman is his wife."

"Then why were they hanging him? What had he done?"

"He attacked the leader of the bandits to protect his wife."

"And that is all?"

"That is all."

The lieutenant shook his head unbelievingly.

MacCorkindale asked, "What will you do with them?"

"They will be shot."

MacCorkindale was silent a moment. At last he asked, "And what will you do with us?"

"You are under arrest, Señor. You and the others. You will have to come with us. My *comandante* will decide what is to be done with you."

"But those Apaches still have the woman. It is my duty to rescue her."

The lieutenant gave him a small, skeptical smile. "With only three men, Señor? Surely you make a jest."

MacCorkindale said wearily, "It's no joke, Lieutenant. We've followed them several hundred miles. We didn't do that for nothing." The Mexican lieutenant looked puzzled. MacCorkindale realized he had just spoken in English. He immediately translated what he had said.

The Mexican turned and issued a sharp command. The three bandits were prodded to the far side of the fire. Their hands were bound and they were told to kneel. They obeyed numbly, as if they knew what was in store for them.

MacCorkindale protested, "Don't they get a trial?"

"A trial? Of what use is a trial? We know who they are and what they have done. We have been hunting them for days."

"But—"

The Mexican lieutenant asked, "Did they give your guide a trial, Lieutenant?" He turned his head. Behind the three kneeling, bound bandits stood three Mexican troopers, each with a rifle in his hands. The lieutenant said, "Fire!"

The three rifles belched black powder-smoke. The bandits were driven forward from their kneeling position to fall face downward on the ground, the tops of their heads half blown away. They lay there, motionless except for a slight twitching of arms or legs, in a somewhat curled-up position because they had been kneeling when they fell.

The Mexican leader turned briskly away from them. The troopers who had executed the three dragged them away out of the circle of firelight.

The venison that Neisha had earlier put on to cook was burned to a crisp except for what the bandits had eaten. Now she began to slice more off the carcass. She cut off only enough for Canavan, Hurley, MacCorkindale and herself, and then went to the fire. Canavan looked at the Mexican lieutenant. "Help yourself, Lieutenant. It's a Mexican deer."

The Mexican lieutenant looked puzzled. MacCorkindale translated, carefully softening Canavan's sarcasm.

The lieutenant issued orders to his men to bivouac. There appeared to be a full troop of perhaps forty or fifty men. Their uniforms were dusty and faded, their faces unshaven, testifying to the pace they had maintained trying to catch the bandits.

The troopers built fires and hacked up the deer carcass. Although Canavan had difficulty swallowing when Neisha brought food to him, for it hurt excruciatingly every time he tried, he forced himself to eat. When he had finished he glanced at MacCorkindale and asked, "What's he going to do with us?"

"He says we are under arrest. He is going to take us back to wherever his headquarters are. He says his *comandante* will decide what is to be done with us."

"And what will that be?"

MacCorkindale shrugged. "Hell, I don't know. They'll probably keep us in the guardhouse a while and then send us back to the States."

"And we'll lose track of Chavo and his band. We'll lose any chance we might have of getting Edith away from them."

"That's about it."

"Can't you talk him into helping us?"

"I tried, but I didn't have any luck."

"Then try again."

"All right. But let's wait until after he eats. Maybe he'll be in a better mood."

Exhausted from his ordeal, Canavan lay down and closed his eyes. Neisha sat nearby, watching him.

He slept almost immediately, but he awakened in less than a half hour. He sat bolt upright, yelling and groping at his neck for the noose that was there and tightening. He realized at once that he had been dreaming and lay back again. He closed his eyes. He could hear the Mexican troopers talking among themselves. He could smell the cooking venison seasoned with spicy peppers. He could hear MacCorkindale and the Mexican

132

lieutenant talking together in Spanish. He could not understand them and fell asleep again, while the voices of MacCorkindale and the Mexican lieutenant droned on.

MacCorkindale looked at his young Mexican counterpart whose name was Esteban Garcia and said, "Lieutenant, these Apache renegades will not live in Mexico in peace. They killed many peaceful Americans on their way here. I myself saw the bodies of the Flores family—"

"Flores? That name is Mexican."

MacCorkindale nodded. "They were Mexicans living in the United States. The Apaches killed them all, even the little ones."

"Why did they take this woman away from you?"

MacCorkindale shrugged. "Who knows why an Apache does anything? I suppose they took her to use as a hostage in case the Army caught up with them."

"Then they have no further use for her."

"No. Except as a slave"

"This woman. She is young?"

MacCorkindale nodded.

"And is she beautiful?"

MacCorkindale remembered Edith Thorne. He nodded. "She is very beautiful."

"She is your woman, Lieutenant?"

"Not yet. But perhaps—"

Lieutenant Garcia's expression softened. He said, "You have come a long way to turn back empty-handed."

MacCorkindale said, "If we do not follow now, the trail will be lost by the time we can return."

"What would you have done when you caught up with the renegades?"

"We could have done nothing. We had only hoped we might get help from the Mexican authorities."

Garcia was silent for a long time, frowning thoughtfully. At last he nodded. "We will follow these renegades, Lieutenant. We will follow them at dawn."

MacCorkindale realized he was grinning foolishly with relief. He seized Garcia's hand and pumped it up and down enthusiastically. He hurried to Canavan and awakened him. "He's going with us, Canavan. He's going to help."

NINETEEN

AT DAWN, LIEUTENANT GARCIA ORDERED THE executed bandits buried. There was no ceremony and immediately afterward the command set out following the Apache renegades. Canavan, MacCorkindale, Hurley and Neisha were permitted to ride at the column's head. By now it was evident to Canavan that the Apaches believed they were safe. They were traveling more slowly than before, and had even sent out hunting parties for deer, as he calculated from the bones and scraps left where the Indians had made camp.

The trail led higher and higher into the mountains. Once Canavan asked Lieutenant Garcia, with MacCorkindale translating, "Are you familiar with these mountains, Lieutenant?"

"Si."

"Have Apaches lived in them before?"

"Si, Señor. There is an Apache stronghold about fifteen miles ahead of us. There is water, and grass, and the valley is surrounded by mountains so that it is defensible."

"And you figure that's where they've gone?"

"Si."

"They don't know anybody is following them. If we're careful, we might be able to jump them before they even know we're here."

"Won't that endanger the white woman you wish to rescue from them? Will they not kill her the moment they are attacked?"

"I want to go into their camp before you attack. I want to try and get her safely out."

"That is suicide, Señor. There are more than thirty Indian braves in the band ahead of us. Besides, if you are caught, the Apaches will be warned and I will lose more men in the attack."

"Not necessarily. They know I have been following them. I was in their camp before."

"Why did you not rescue the woman then?"

"She panicked. But I don't think she'll do it again. Let me go ahead and scout, Lieutenant. I'll come back and report as soon as I have located them."

Lieutenant Garcia hesitated. Then he nodded.

Canavan reached out and touched Neisha's hand. He smiled at her. He could see she was exhausted, but she did not complain. She returned his smile and he forged ahead of the column, climbing steeply now along the Apaches' trail.

He felt as though he had been following this trail for months. His whole body ached. His neck, scraped raw by the rope, was lightly scabbed but it still burned, still hurt when anything rubbed against it. He held himself in a peculiarly stiff-necked attitude, trying to spare himself as much pain as possible.

He had a feeling that this would be over soon. They would either rescue Edith or they would cause her death. But there could be no turning back. If they turned back she would die anyway. If the Apaches didn't kill her outright, they'd work or starve her to death.

Lieutenant Garcia had said the Apache stronghold was fifteen miles ahead. It was well past noon. Canavan climbed steadily, but slowly, saving his horse and himself, not wanting to arrive before dusk.

He kept his attention on the trail, sometimes dismounting to study it. The Apaches had passed this way more than a day before so he needn't worry about an ambush. All that need concern him was the possibility that they had sentries out.

The afternoon wore steadily away. Once he thought about the two bounty hunters and wondered briefly if they had found Healey's grave and dug his body up. He grimaced with distaste, thinking about it.

When he guessed he had gone two-thirds of the distance to the Apache camp, he left the trail, which followed a dry watercourse, and climbed the mountain slope rising on his left, crossing over the first ridge as soon as he could. He stayed in ravines and low places not only because they were brushy and afforded cover, but because he knew how far a man can be seen when he is silhouetted against the sky.

The sun sank steadily toward the horizon. A few high clouds flamed in its dying glow and soon thereafter dusk crept across the land. In the last, fading light Canavan crested the last ridge separating him from the Indian camp.

He backed away from it as soon as he saw the fires winking in the narrow valley below. He tied his horse in a heavy clump of mesquite then returned to his vantage point. He lay down and watched the Indian camp carefully, searching for Edith Thorne.

136

There were squaws in camp, and children, the families of the renegades. He admitted that it was possible they had taken Edith's original clothes away from her. They would have replaced them with their own castoffs. Satisfied that there was no woman down there dressed in the clothes of a white woman, he began to look for a ragged squaw. But at last he was forced to give up. The distance was too great.

Now he counted the Indians carefully, passing over children and those he could tell were squaws. He counted twenty-nine he was sure were men. He supposed there might be from two to half a dozen out hunting, scouting or standing guard. That would put the total of Apache braves at about thirty-five.

He had the information he needed, but he lingered, still hoping he would spot Edith Thorne. Finally, two hours after dark, he gave up. He eased back away from the ridge top, found his horse in the clump of mesquite, and led him back toward the place where the Mexican troops had camped.

It was almost midnight when he arrived. Most of the troopers were asleep. He called out to the first sentry he encountered and walked into camp, leading his horse. Most of the fires had died. MacCorkindale, Neisha and Hurley sat beside one of the few that had not. All three turned their heads when they heard him approach.

Lieutenant Garcia, also awake, came striding toward him. He asked a question in Spanish, which MacCorkindale translated. "Did you see her?"

Canavan shook his head. "But I was over a quarter of a mile away. There are squaws and children with them and they have probably taken away her clothes. She'd be dressed like any squaw, only maybe more ragged than the others are."

MacCorkindale translated and Garcia frowned. "She has probably been killed. That is why you could not see her in their camp."

Canavan shrugged. He knew it was possible that Edith Thorne was dead. But he had to know for sure. So did MacCorkindale. He said, "Lieutenant MacCorkindale, you've got to persuade him to attack that camp at dawn. Neither you nor I will be able to rest until we know if she's alive or not."

MacCorkindale spoke earnestly in Spanish. The Mexican Lieutenant looked doubtful. MacCorkindale continued persuasively. Garcia, frowning, began to pace nervously back and forth.

Canavan asked, "What did he say?"

"He hasn't made up his mind. He says if she is in that camp, they will kill her when he attacks. He says if she is not there, then it is useless to attack."

"Tell him what those Apaches will do to the Mexicans that live nearby. Tell him what they did to the Flores family."

"He knows, but I'll tell him again." MacCorkindale turned again to Garcia. Canavan heard the word "Flores" spoken several times. Finally MacCorkindale reported to Canavan. "He says not many families live in this area. He says he will lose many men."

"Well for God's sake! Tell him he's a *soldier*. Tell him these are hostile Indians that have killed many peaceful settlers and will kill many more. Tell him if he does not attack them now and drive them north or capture them, he will have to attack them later. The United States government is certain to contact the Mexican government and ask them to help."

MacCorkindale spoke to Garcia again. At last Garcia nodded reluctantly. MacCorkindale said, "He says he will attack. He says he will try to capture the Indians and if he does he will escort them north and turn them over to the Americans. But he says they will most certainly kill Edith when they are attacked and he wants it understood that he assumes no responsibility for her death."

Canavan said, "Tell him to rouse his men. I will lead him to the Apache camp. If he leaves within an hour, he can get there and surround it by dawn."

"What about Edith? He's right when he says they'll kill her."

"I know it. I'm going in before he attacks. Maybe I can find her in time and maybe I can't. But it's the only chance she's got. If we don't get her they'll kill her anyway."

MacCorkindale looked at Neisha, sitting quietly by the fire. "Her brother is one of those renegades. What is she going to think about our attacking them?"

Canavan said, "She'll grieve if he's killed, of course. But to an Apache, fighting is an accepted part of life."

He walked to the fire and squatted beside Neisha. He reached out and took her hand in his own. "The Mexicans are going to attack the Apaches at dawn."

She nodded.

"Chavo may be killed," he went on.

"He is a warrior."

"I am going into their camp to look for Edith Thorne."

She nodded.

"I want you to go with me. I need your help. I do not want to alert the Indians. If the lieutenant is able to surprise them, fewer on both sides will be killed."

"I will go with you." But there was a frown on her normally smooth forehead.

He said, "Perhaps the lieutenant will marry Edith Thorne. But I will not."

"Chavo will be put into the white man's jail if he is not killed. The others will go back to the reservation. You will be in no danger from Apaches then. You will not need me any more."

For a moment he couldn't speak. He felt more ashamed than ever in his life. He should have realized that she understood his motives in marrying her, but he never had. Not until now.

He turned and took her face between his hands. He said, "I took you from the reservation because you were Chavo's sister. But I have changed since then. I have learned to love you. No matter what happens to Chavo's renegades, I want you to stay with me. We will return home by way of Tucson. We will be married in the Christian church."

Tears suddenly filled her eyes. He put his arms around her and held her close, scarcely aware of the confusion in camp as the Mexican bugler roused the troops.

Releasing her, he got his razor out of his saddlebags. He shaved his heavy growth of whiskers off, using firelight and a small piece of broken mirror he carried with his razor and shaving soap. If he was going into the Apache camp he didn't want a beard giving him away. He got a piece of red cloth from Neisha and tied it around his head in the Apache way. His hair was too short and it wasn't black. But he might pass a casual inspection in the darkness. At least he wouldn't stand out.

The troopers fell in, mounted and ready to go. Canavan and Neisha led off. There was no need to trail. Canavan knew the way. The troop of Mexican cavalry strung out behind. Garcia and MacCorkindale rode directly behind Neisha and Canavan. Canavan didn't see Hurley, but he supposed he was somewhere near MacCorkindale.

His stomach felt as if it had knots in it. His chest was tight. Everything was committed now, Garcia's troop of cavalry, he and Hurley and MacCorkindale. Most of all, Edith Thorne's life was irrevocably committed. Dawn would decide whether she was to live or die.

He tried to remember her face and couldn't. Nor, could he recall her voice. It was as if she were already dead. He put all thought of her temporarily out of his mind. The column plodded along through the night, less than silently, but probably not audible for more than a quarter mile. A thin line of gray was becoming visible along the horizon in the east when they finally reached a point beyond which Canavan dared not go. He stopped, and when Garcia and MacCorkindale caught up, he pointed to the ridges on both sides. "Tell him to deploy a third of his force to the right, a third to the left. I don't want to tell him how to fight this battle, but if the two flanking forces were to get beyond and above the Apache camp, then the third force could drive the Indians up the valley into them."

MacCorkindale translated the battle plan to Lieutenant Garcia, who nodded agreement with it and immediately called back the necessary orders to implement it.

Canavan said, "Tell him not to attack until it's light enough to shoot. That ought to give me about twenty minutes, which is about all the time I'll need."

MacCorkindale called, "Good luck, Mr. Canavan."

Canavan grinned thinly at him, a grin he knew MacCorkindale couldn't see. He said, "Same to you,

141

Lieutenant," and rode away up the rocky valley with Neisha silently following.

TWENTY

TIME WAS SHORT AND CANAVAN HEADED STRAIGHT up the canyon. It was a calculated risk, but he hoped that if they were discovered, it would be assumed they belonged with the party of Apache renegades. He kept glancing worriedly toward the east, at the spreading line of gray. A couple of times he glanced at Neisha's face, wondering what she was thinking, what her expression was, but it was too dark to tell.

Half a mile from where they had left the troopers, they rounded a turn in the canyon and saw the Apache camp ahead. There were only a couple of fires burning now. All the rest had died to beds of glowing coals.

Canavan swung from his horse and whispered to Neisha to dismount. She obeyed, and he led the two horses away from the road into the concealment of some head-high rocks. He tied them securely and began to jog up the valley toward the Apache camp.

He had seen perhaps a dozen wickiups from the hillside earlier. He could not yet make out their outlines, but he supposed Edith was in one of them. To Neisha trotting tirelessly and silently at his side, he said, "Try and find her, but I don't want you in this camp when the Mexican troops attack. They won't be able to tell you from the others in the excitement. Meet me on the far side as soon as it is light."

"I want to stay with you."

He agreed, obscurely relieved that they would not be separated. He might even have a better chance of

142

finding Edith if Neisha stayed with him. And he would be with her when the Mexican troops attacked. He would be able to protect her from them.

They were near the Apache camp now, less than a hundred yards away. Caravan stopped to catch his breath. He stared at the village, becoming visible in the first light of dawn. The whole sky now was gray. He glanced right and left at the rocky hillsides, half expecting to hear sounds from the Mexican troops, surprised when he did not. For a chilling instant he wondered if Lieutenant Garcia had changed his mind.

He shook his head impatiently. The Mexicans were not recruits. They were experienced border troops. They had fought Indians, and bandits, and they were too tough and smart to give their presence away before the time arrived for the attack.

A dozen wickiups to search. No more than twenty minutes to do it in without light, risking discovery in each of them—He shook his head almost imperceptibly. That method was too cumbersome, too risky and too slow. He whispered to Neisha, "I'm going to grab one of them. I'm going to make him tell me where she is."

Neisha did not reply. He could faintly see her face now and he could see the tension in it. He moved forward immediately.

Sleeping braves were lumped shapes near the fires. Only families lived in wickiups so far, he thought. There had been time for only the most hasty kind of construction, none for building wickiups to shelter unmarried men.

He spotted an Indian sitting cross-legged on the ground beside one of the fires at the left side of the village. He swerved and ran toward him, drawing his knife as he did. He came up behind the man, without

143

attracting notice until he was less than a few feet away. The man turned his head and Caravan closed the distance between them with a rush. He circled the man's neck with his arm, closing his windpipe, and placed the knife against his throat just beneath his chin. In Apache he whispered, "Make a sound and you are dead! Where is the white captive? In which wickiup?"

The Apache made no sound. Caravan loosened his strangling arm a little and asked, "Where?"

The man shook his head. Caravan let the point of the knife draw blood from the Indian's throat and for the third time asked, "Where?"

Instead of answering, the Indian opened his mouth to yell a warning to the others. Caravan choked the cry off savagely.

The Indian began struggling. His hand went to his waist where his own knife hung and closed over its grip.

Canavan had no choice. In an instant the Indian's knife would be buried in him. He cut the Apache's throat and flung him away. The knife in the Indian's hand made a vicious, splashing arc and the point raked Canavan's shirt, drawing blood from his chest beneath.

He ran toward the nearest wickiup, cursing savagely to himself. Damn Apaches anyway! They hated whites so fiercely they would rather die than tell a white man anything. The brave whose throat he had cut lay thrashing not far from the fire, sure to attract attention if he didn't stop kicking soon.

Neisha ducked into the wickiup, motioning silently for him to remain outside. He stood there by the entrance, staring with something close to horror at the dying Indian, whose struggles now were weakening. So far, nobody had noticed him; but that wasn't too surprising. Only two or three of the others were awake and they happened to be facing the other way. The dying Indian was making scarcely any sound because his windpipe had been cut.

He heard talking inside the wickiup, but it was too muffled for him to make out the words. An instant later, Neisha emerged, shaking her head at him. They moved on to the next wickiup, and again Neisha disappeared inside.

It was now almost fully light. The sleeping Indians were stirring. The one whose throat Canavan had cut was dead.

A brave stumbled toward the fire, rubbing sleep from his eyes. He saw the dead Indian and saw the blood. He turned and roared out a startled warning to the others. Immediately the wickiups began disgorging their occupants. Neisha came out of the second wickiup followed by an angry squaw. Canavan grasped her arm and pulled her around in back of it. The squaw followed, shrieking at them both.

Canavan glanced desperately at the hillsides. He saw the uniforms of the Mexican troopers now. They were close enough, within rifle shot. At the same time he heard the bugle down the canyon and an instant later Lieutenant Garcia, sabre drawn, came thundering into sight followed by MacCorkindale, Hurley and more than a dozen of his men.

The Apaches, startled and for an instant bewildered, seized weapons and turned to meet the oncoming Mexicans. As they did, the troopers on both hillsides began firing. One fallen Apache crawled to the shelter of a wickiup, dragging a broken leg behind. Another threw out his arms and fell, shot in the chest, and thereafter lay completely still.

No time now to search the other wickiups. Canavan

lifted his head and roared, "Edith! Wherever you are, run! Edith! Run!"

Desperately he cast his glance back and forth. Indians were everywhere, men, women, children, caught up in panic at the attack. The troopers on the hillsides continued to pour deadly rifle fire into the camp. Those under Garcia were now within two hundred yards and in moments would come thundering through the Apache village.

Canavan bawled, "Edith! Damn it, where are you?"

He glanced at Neisha, hesitating, trying to make a decision that was agonizing to make. Every instant she was in this camp, Neisha was in deadly peril, both from the Indians and from the Mexicans who would probably not be able to distinguish between her and the other Apache women in the excitement of the attack. They had come so far to rescue Edith and now that she was so close. He glanced at Neisha, then glanced at the uproar in the Apache camp. He had only seconds to make up his mind.

He grabbed Neisha's arm. "Come on! I'm not going to have you killed while I look for her!" He dragged her toward the upper edge of the village, and she ran like a deer now, forging a few feet ahead but glancing behind every now and then to be certain he was following.

So far, neither of them had attracted the attention of the Apaches, who were too occupied with the Mexican troops attacking from three sides. But suddenly, several of the Apache braves noticed them and shouted with outrage that they had penetrated the camp and were escaping from it. A bullet tugged at Canavan's shirt. The muzzle blast from another Apache gun seared the side of his face with burning grains of powder and almost blinded him. Suddenly he was not thinking of

146

himself, or even of Neisha but of the Flores family, husband, wife, children, babies, wantonly slain by these same Apache braves.

He stopped, knelt, and brought his revolver to bear on the closest of the Indians. He fired and saw the man driven back by the force of the heavy slug. He fired again and saw another Indian go down. Neisha came running back. She stopped beside him, pulling at his arm, screaming, "Jason! Jason, come on! The soldiers—"

The battle was now a steady roar. There was the thunder of the Mexican troopers' horses as they pounded through the Apache camp. There were their hoarse shouts, and the shouted orders of Lieutenant Garcia. There were the cries of the Apaches, of the women, of the terrified children, of enraged and savage men.

And there was the gunfire, steady and continuous and the acrid smelling powder smoke, a blue-gray cloud that hung over everything.

Less than a minute had passed since Canavan roared at Edith Thorne to run if she could. Now, suddenly, he saw her. She had emerged from one of the wickiups, so incredibly filthy she was scarcely recognizable. But he had seen her once before in this condition, hair matted, clothes greasy and ragged, face cruelly sunburned and blistered, scabbed where the blisters had broken and began to heal.

She glanced frantically to right and left as she ran, and Canavan bawled at her, "Edith! This way!"

A squaw was behind her, pursuing her, with a knife in hand. Canavan instantly knew that the squaw had orders to kill her if she tried to escape. Now the squaw was steadily closing the distance separating them. When it appeared inevitable that the squaw would catch and kill her, Canavan no longer had a choice. He raised his revolver and sighted carefully at the running squaw. If he missed, Edith would be dead before he could take aim and shoot again, because by then he would be afraid to shoot at the squaw for fear of hitting Edith by mistake.

He fired and the squaw collapsed in a crumpled heap. Edith reached him, stumbling and falling as she did. Canavan yanked her to her feet and dragged her toward the upper end of the camp. Neisha grabbed her other arm and between them they literally forced her to run, to keep up with them. Canavan didn't dare look behind. He prayed that none of the Apaches was taking aim at them. He prayed that they could reach shelter before the Mexican troopers caught up with them.

Less than a hundred yards beyond the last wickiup, Canavan dragged Edith into the brushy creek bottom and forced her to the ground. He yelled, "Stay there!" and turned, his revolver in his hand.

He could hear Neisha talking to Edith, trying to calm her hysteria. He saw Garcia, MacCorkindale, Hurley and the Mexican troopers regrouping this side of the Apache camp preparatory to making still another charge back through it. On both sides, other Mexican troopers were descending from the mountain slopes, firing as they came. Canavan yelled, "MacCorkindale! Hurley! Over here!"

The pair turned their heads, saw him, and trotted their horses toward him. Canavan yelled, "I've got her! She's right here, safe!"

MacCorkindale swung from his horse, handing the reins to Hurley, who remained mounted, revolver in hand, facing the Apache camp watchfully. He knelt beside Edith and took her in his arms.

Surprisingly, there were tears in MacCorkindale's eyes, tears that spilled over and ran across his bearded cheeks. He held her gently, patting her back awkwardly and speaking comforting words. Over and over he said, "It's all right, Ma'am. It's over now and you're safe. It's all right, Ma'am."

Canavan realized that the firing had stopped. Staring toward the Apache camp, he saw that the Indians had thrown down their arms. They stood with hands raised, surrendering.

He took an instant to touch Neisha's face and to smile at her. Then he ran back to the village, pulling the red band of cloth from around his head. Garcia said something in Spanish that Canavan couldn't understand, but he understood that Garcia wanted the Apaches to move to one side of the camp while his soldiers gathered up their arms. Canavan reissued the order in Apache and watched them sullenly obey.

MacCorkindale approached, an arm around Edith Thorne. He translated the Mexican lieutenant's further instructions to the Apaches, and Canavan translated into the Apache tongue.

The sun poked its blazing rim above the mountains to the east. Garcia spoke to MacCorkindale, who said to Canavan, "He says he will escort the Apache prisoners to the border and hold them there until I can bring the troops from Fort Chiricahua."

Canavan nodded.

MacCorkindale smiled faintly, "I'll get my captain's bars out of this instead of getting cashiered for losing Miss Thorne to the Indians."

Canavan nodded.

MacCorkindale said, "I owe it all to you. We both owe it all to you."

149

Canavan said, "Goodbye, Edith."

"Goodbye." Her voice was cracked and hoarse, but he could detect no regret in it.

He looked at Neisha. "If we're going to stop in Tucson and get married in the church, we'd better be on our way."

She gave him one of her rare, warm smiles. Walking, they headed down the canyon toward the place they had left their horses earlier.

We hope that you enjoyed reading this
Sagebrush Large Print Western.
If you would like to read more Sagebrush titles,
ask your librarian or contact the Publishers:

United States and Canada

Thomas T. Beeler, *Publisher*
Post Office Box 659
Hampton Falls, New Hampshire 03844-0659
(800) 818-7574

United Kingdom, Eire, and
the Republic of South Africa

Isis Publishing Ltd
7 Centremead
Osney Mead
Oxford OX2 0ES England
(01865) 250333

Australia and New Zealand

Bolinda Publishing Pty. Ltd.
17 Mohr Street
Tullamarine, 3043, Victoria, Australia
(016103) 9338 0666